Johnny Jihad

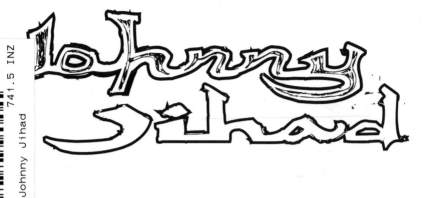

Johnny Jihad

Story and art by Ryan Inzana
Back cover by Brian Hogan and Ryan Inzana
Additional design by Jack Aguirre

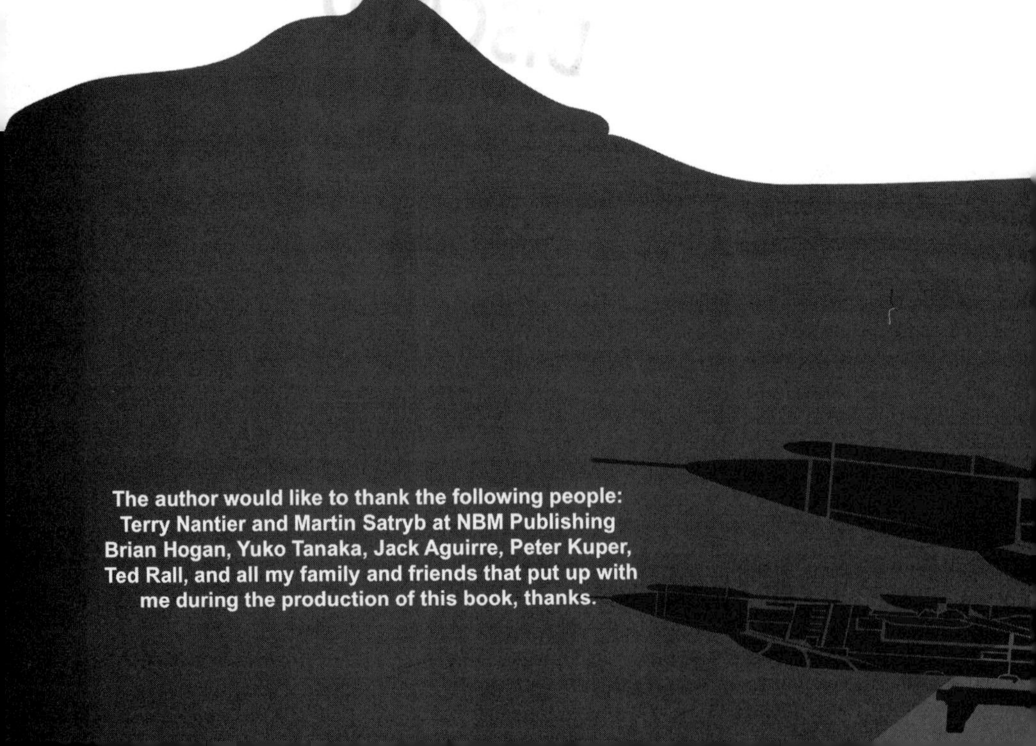

The author would like to thank the following people:
Terry Nantier and Martin Satryb at NBM Publishing
Brian Hogan, Yuko Tanaka, Jack Aguirre, Peter Kuper,
Ted Rall, and all my family and friends that put up with
me during the production of this book, thanks.

This book is dedicated to Rose Tuccillo

The Basis of Inspiration

In November of 2001, John Walker Lindh was taken into custody after a Taliban uprising at a prison compound in Mazar-e-Sharif. A stunned nation, still coming to grips with the horrors that occurred in New York City and Washington on September 11th, watched in disbelief as a young, *white*, American boy was carted away by CIA officers. The media, and the administration as well, had done a pretty good job of painting a middle-eastern face on this new enemy in a "crusade" to wage war against terrorism. But here was John Walker Lindh, a white-boy from Marin County, California, now a member of an ambiguous group of "evil-doers" over in Afghanistan.

The initial shock the nation felt after seeing Lindh apprehended didn't last long, it was soon business as usual. Attorney General John Ashcroft had nearly every man of middle-eastern origin registering themselves with the INS, a move so bold, the thought of Nazis rounding up Jews in World War II immediately comes to mind. The American 5-minute consciousness of John Walker Lindh had been deleted from the hard-drive. And as the National Alert system fluctuates between yellow and orange, the media constantly harangues us to keep an eye out for "suspicious looking individuals," in other words, any Arab posting a letter (it could be Anthrax, folks.) Who would think that the young, white, disassociated teenager standing right next to you could have a fertilizer bomb in the trunk of his 2003 Volkswagen Jetta?

Which brings me to Johnny Jihad, a fictional tale, based on real people and real events that have nothing to do with John Walker Lindh. As amazed as the public was upon first hearing of "the American Taliban," it shouldn't have been such a surprise, not to a country that has hosted Islamic extremist "terror" organizations for 20 years.

As early as 1982, an organization known as Medhtab al-Khadamat (MAK) had established training grounds in Afghanistan to fight Soviet occupation. These camps were composed mainly of middle-eastern members, such as Pakistanis and Egyptians, but were attracting thousands of recruits from other non-Muslim countries. "Even westerners joined the fight –Muslims and Non-Muslims– including Americans, British, French and Australians. These recruits were initially met with some skepticism, but most applied themselves with merit and were generally accepted."[1]

These camps, while being heavily funded by the Central Intelligence Agency, were a breeding ground for anti-American sentiment. Osama Bin Laden, who co-founded MAK, once said, "I have always hated the Americans because they are against Muslims...We didn't want the US support in Afghanistan, but we just happened to be fighting the same enemy." Nonetheless, American tax dollars funded camps that became a precedent in training a new wave of soldiers for a war that began against the Soviets, but quickly spiraled into a war against Western expansionism. Recruitment offices sprang up in at least 12 US cities, capitalizing on what many saw as a domineering American foreign policy unfairly supporting

Israeli oppression of the Palestinians, and with military bases encroaching on the holy land in Saudi Arabia.

Thus, it was not long before training camps began to appear in America. Recruits trained in Afghan camps would set up small, isolated compounds that mimicked the training of the Afghan camps. One such camp that has been included on a State Department's list of terror organizations is Jamaat Ul Fuqra; also know as Tanzeem Ul Fuqra. "Jamaat ul-Fuqra is an Islamic sect that seeks to purify Islam through violence. Fuqra is led by Pakistani cleric Shaykh Mubarik Ali Gilani, who established the organization in the early 1980s. Gilani now resides in Pakistan, but most Fuqra cells are located in North America."[2]

Sheikh Gilani was the man *Wall Street Journal* reporter Daniel Pearl reportedly went to meet when he disappeared in Karachi, Pakistan Jan. 23rd, 2001. He has apparent links to "shoe bomber" Richard C. Reid as well as training compounds in New York, Michigan, South Carolina, California, Colorado and perhaps other states.

On February 13, 2003, NBC News reported: "FBI sources say 20 to 40 militant Muslims inside this country are believed to have STRONG Al Qaeda connections." These estimates evidently do not include Fuqra members, which Sheikh Gilani said has "thousands of American followers."

The investigation into Sheikh Gilani and the Fuqra camps has received little to no publicity. There has also been a blatant disregard of the matter by American officials. The link between Sheikh Gilani and Osama Bin Laden seems to be more than a loose connection. A reporter who was able to obtain an interview with the elusive Sheikh said, "I was taken to him by one of bin Laden's closest friends, a former intelligence officer from Pakistan."[3]

Organizations like Al Qaeda and Jamaat Ul Fuqra are often very enticing to young, disenfranchised youth in Middle-Eastern countries as well as in the United States. In a western culture, such as America's, that thoroughly embraces violence through movies, TV and video games, a prospective Al Qaeda recruit would find the use of violence an appealing factor in joining such an organization. This is a cultural phenomenon which is directly linked to a society that has teenagers engaging in shooting sprees in their high schools. It is a generation of children that sees violence as an acceptable alternative. The peaceful aspects of Islam are underplayed, while extremist indoctrination becomes the selling point to these youths. "Many of these people (Al Qaeda recruits) are younger than before – between 20 and 30."[4]

President Bush believes that only through war can peace be achieved in Iraq, thus setting an example that war is the answer. Ironically, many young jihadists, in the United States and abroad, believe in that exact same thing.

Ryan Inzana
New York, 2003

[1] Robinson, Adam, *Bin Laden: Behind The Mask of Terror* New York: Arcade Publishing 2001.
[2] U.S. DEPARTMENT OF STATE 1997 APRIL: PATTERNS OF GLOBAL TERRORISM, 1996 Office of the Coordinator for Counter-terrorism, Philip C. Wilcox, Jr.
[3] *60 Minutes II, CBS* News (September 2002).
[4] Don Van Natta, Jr. and Desmond Butler, "Anger on Iraq Seen as New Qaeda Recruiting Tool," *New York Times* (March 16, 2003).

Also available:

To Afghanistan & Back, $15.95
Kafka: Give It Up! & other short stories, $15.95
No Pasaran! Vol.1: $13.95, vol.2: $11.95
Add $3 P&H 1st item, $1 each addt'l

We have over 200 graphic novels in print,
write for our color catalog:
NBM, 555 8th Ave., Suite 1202
New York, NY 10018
www.nbmpublishing.com

ISBN 1-56163-353-4
© 2003 Ryan Inzana

3   2   1

Library of Congress Cataloging-in-Publication Data

Inzana, Ryan.
   Johnny Jihad / by Ryan Inzana.
      p. cm.
   ISBN 1-56163-353-4
   I. Title.

PN6727.I59J64 2003
741.5'973--dc21

                                        2003041219

ComicsLit is an imprint
and trademark of

NANTIER · BEALL · MINOUSTCHINE
Publishing inc.
new york

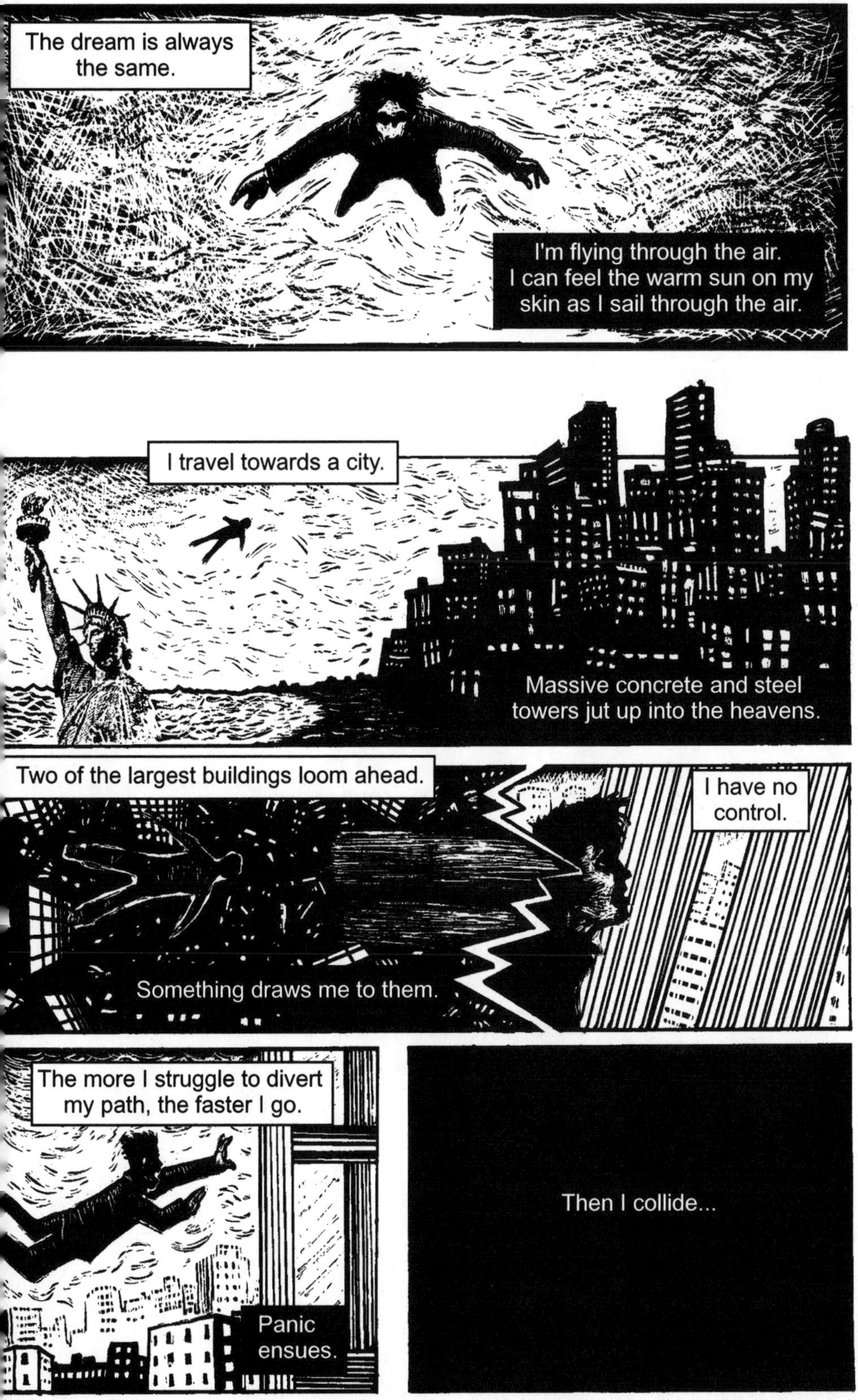
The dream is always the same.
I'm flying through the air. I can feel the warm sun on my skin as I sail through the air.
I travel towards a city.
Massive concrete and steel towers jut up into the heavens.
Two of the largest buildings loom ahead.
Something draws me to them.
I have no control.
The more I struggle to divert my path, the faster I go.
Panic ensues.
Then I collide...

Oct. 25th, 2001

Check, one, two...

Is this thing on?
Check...
My English teacher in high school told me I could be a writer. She told me I had a way with words.
Somewhere on the road of life, things took a serious detour.
This is my first attempt at serious journalism, it also happens to be my life story.
My name is John Sendel of Trenton, NJ, United States of America.
Also known as Abdullah Akbar.
All that's unimportant now.
What's important is that you understand that everything is not my fault, but then again... it is.
Nothing really matters to me, except telling this story, my last will and testament.
Then I can fade from the face of the world.
For all intents and purposes, I already have.
Well, where should I begin?

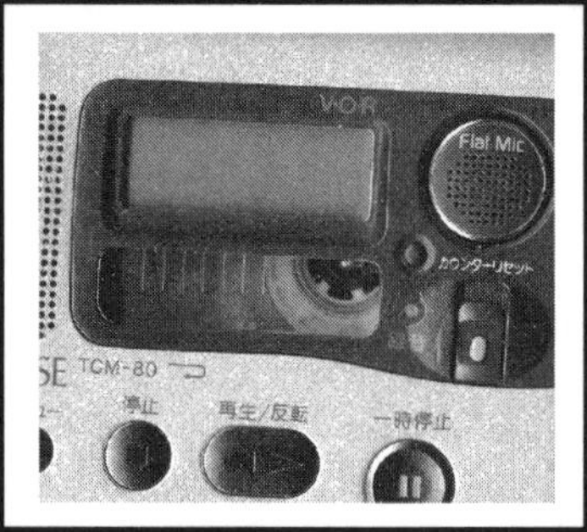
VOR
Flat Mic
TCM-80

Right now, I'm sitting in the bombed out town of Khost, Afghanistan.
A world away from where this story begins.
I'm recording this on a tape deck that somehow avoided destruction by the Taliban, as it is their decree that Western technology should be destroyed.
This recorder was most likely on death row, confiscated as contra-band, awaiting destruction.
That is, before the bombing started.
I'm awaiting my fate.
I couldn't run like the rest, due to this gangrene which has set in on my leg.
So I say to the fighter pilots dropping 20 ton bombs from thousands of feet above:

Here I am

I dare you

Come and get me.

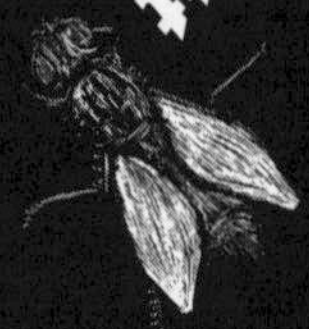

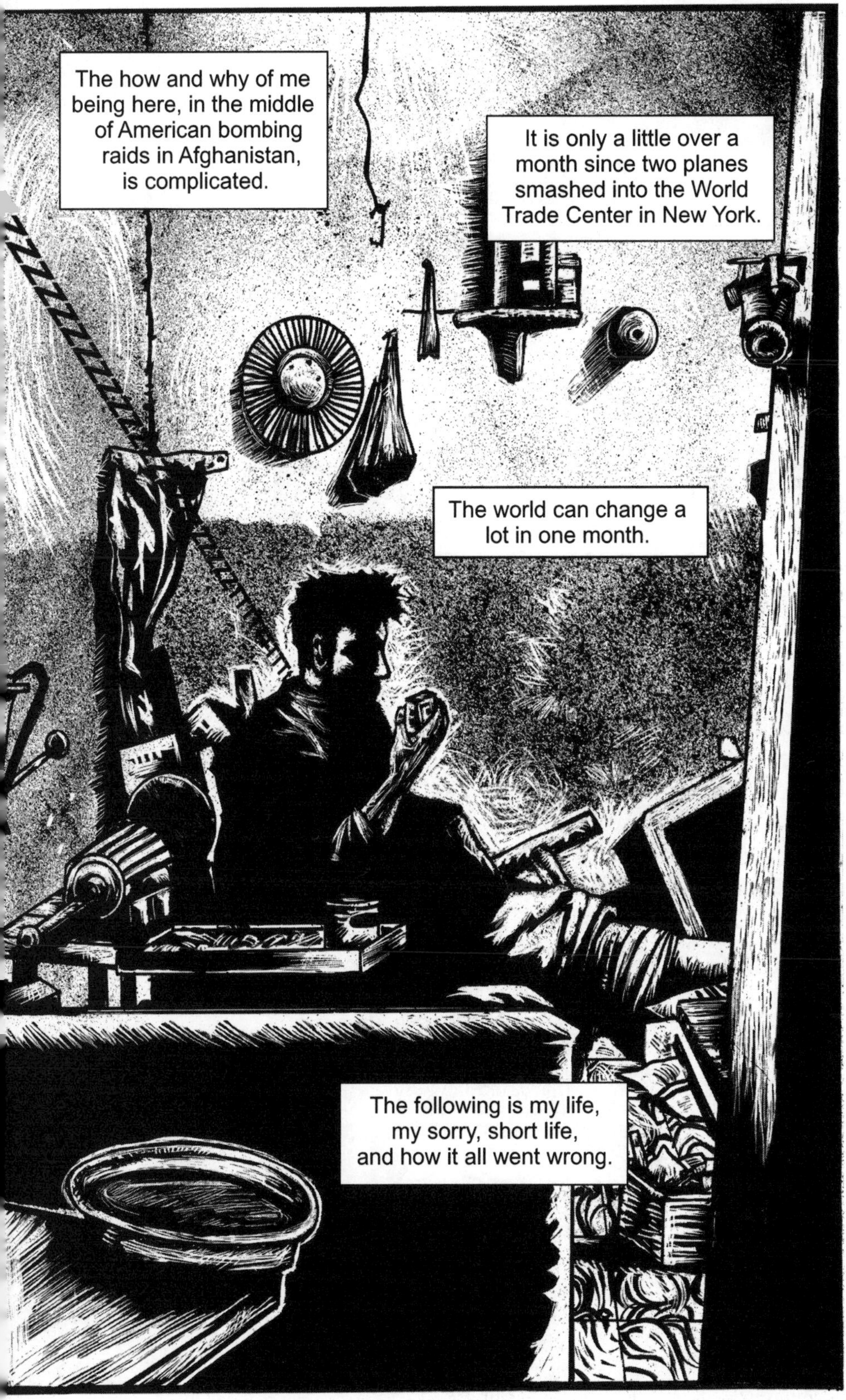
The how and why of me being here, in the middle of American bombing raids in Afghanistan, is complicated.
It is only a little over a month since two planes smashed into the World Trade Center in New York.
The world can change a lot in one month.
The following is my life, my sorry, short life, and how it all went wrong.

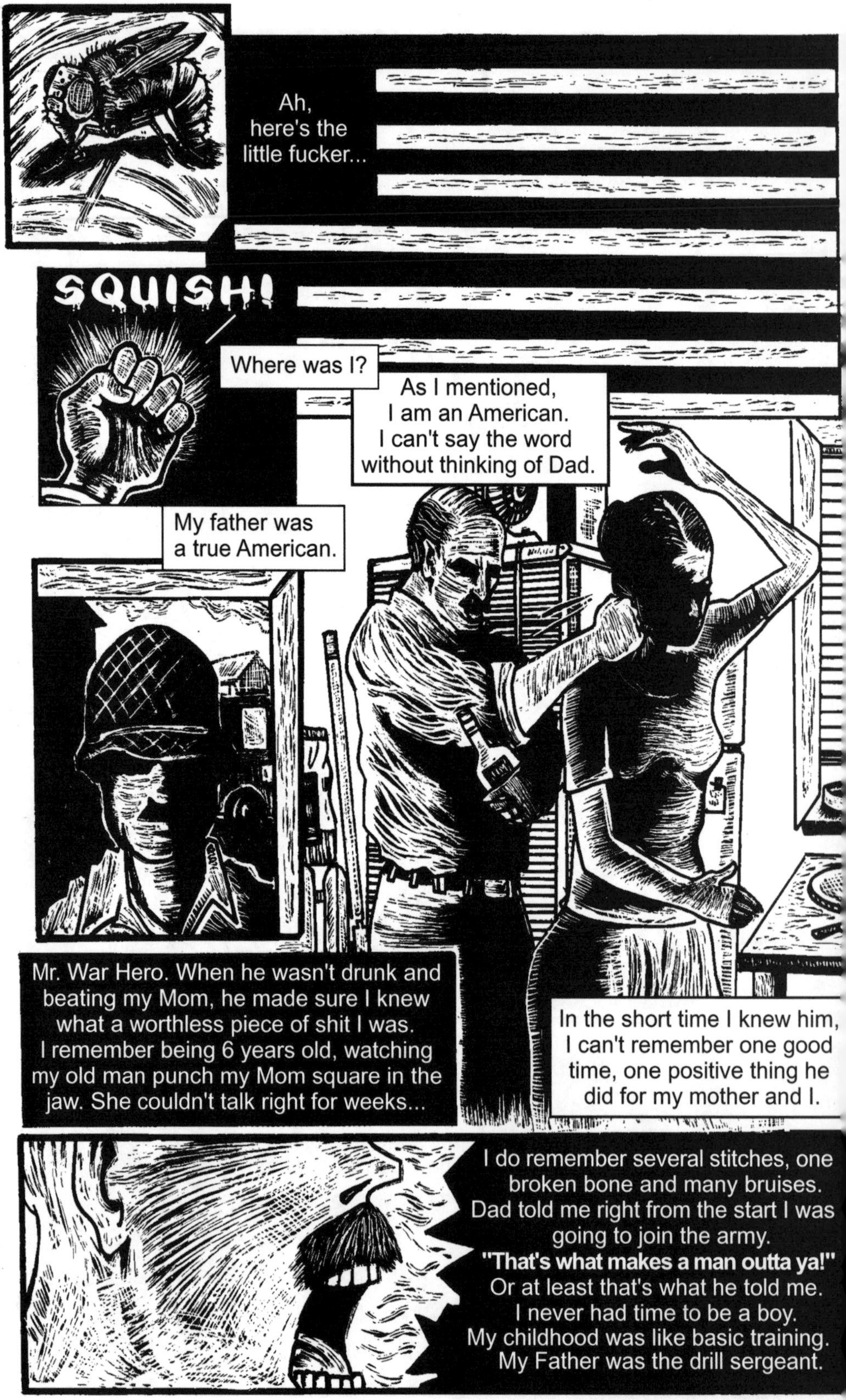
Ah, here's the little fucker...
SQUISH!
Where was I?
As I mentioned, I am an American. I can't say the word without thinking of Dad.
My father was a true American.
Mr. War Hero. When he wasn't drunk and beating my Mom, he made sure I knew what a worthless piece of shit I was. I remember being 6 years old, watching my old man punch my Mom square in the jaw. She couldn't talk right for weeks...
In the short time I knew him, I can't remember one good time, one positive thing he did for my mother and I.
I do remember several stitches, one broken bone and many bruises. Dad told me right from the start I was going to join the army.
"That's what makes a man outta ya!"
Or at least that's what he told me. I never had time to be a boy. My childhood was like basic training. My Father was the drill sergeant.

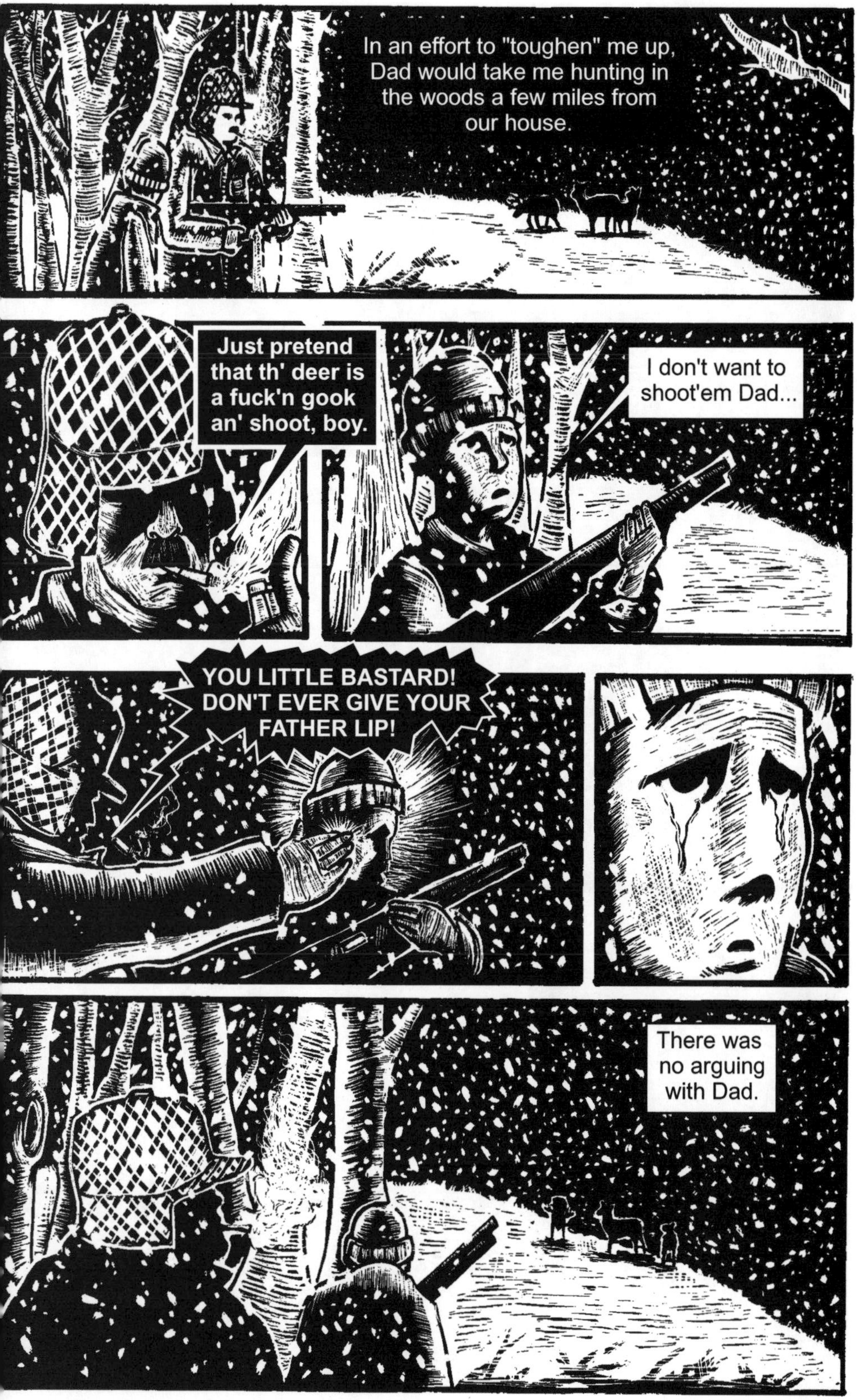
In an effort to "toughen" me up, Dad would take me hunting in the woods a few miles from our house.
Just pretend that th' deer is a fuck'n gook an' shoot, boy.
I don't want to shoot'em Dad...
YOU LITTLE BASTARD! DON'T EVER GIVE YOUR FATHER LIP!
There was no arguing with Dad.

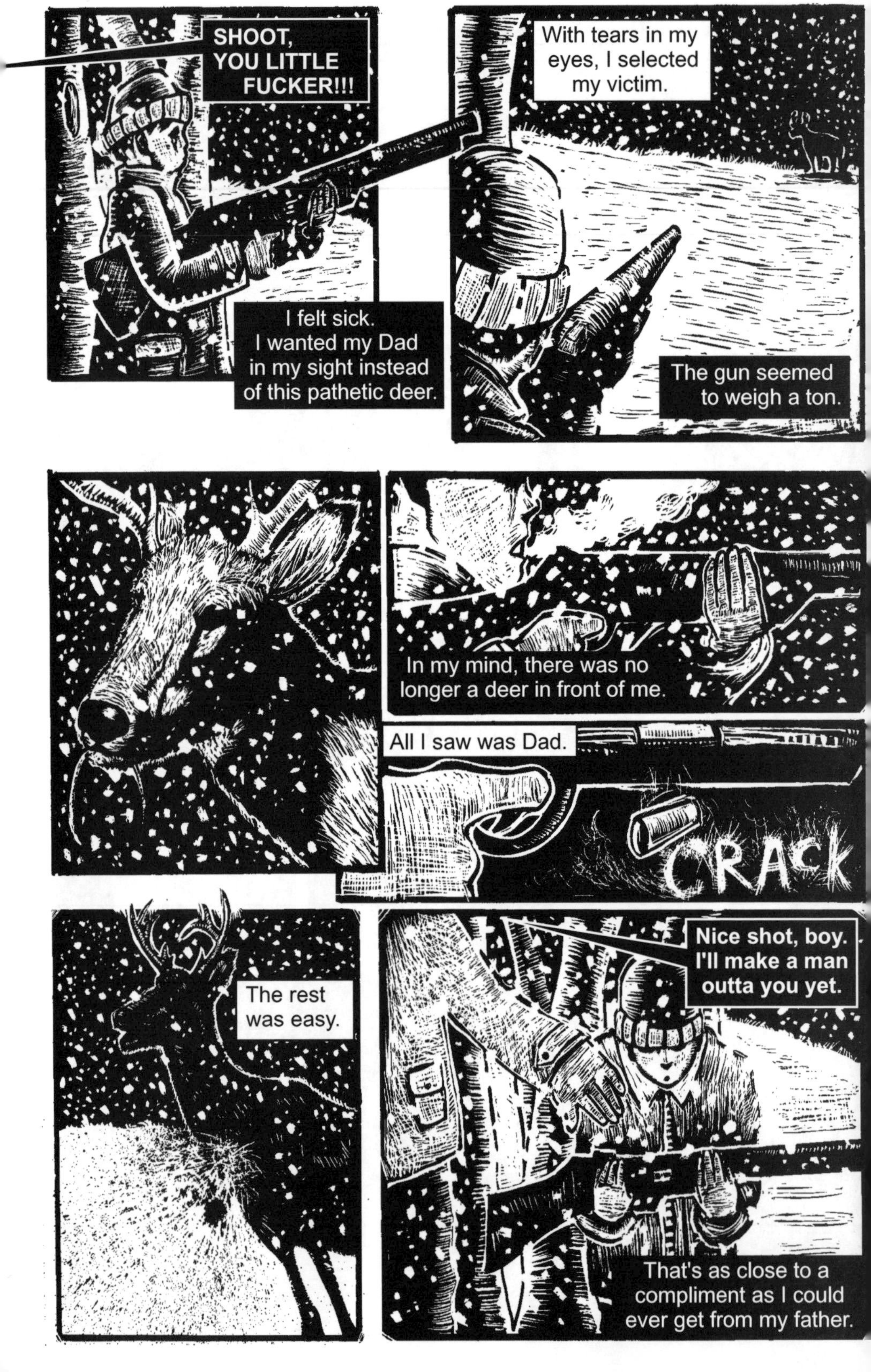
SHOOT, YOU LITTLE FUCKER!!!
I felt sick. I wanted my Dad in my sight instead of this pathetic deer.
With tears in my eyes, I selected my victim.
The gun seemed to weigh a ton.
In my mind, there was no longer a deer in front of me.
All I saw was Dad.
CRACK
The rest was easy.
Nice shot, boy. I'll make a man outta you yet.
That's as close to a compliment as I could ever get from my father.

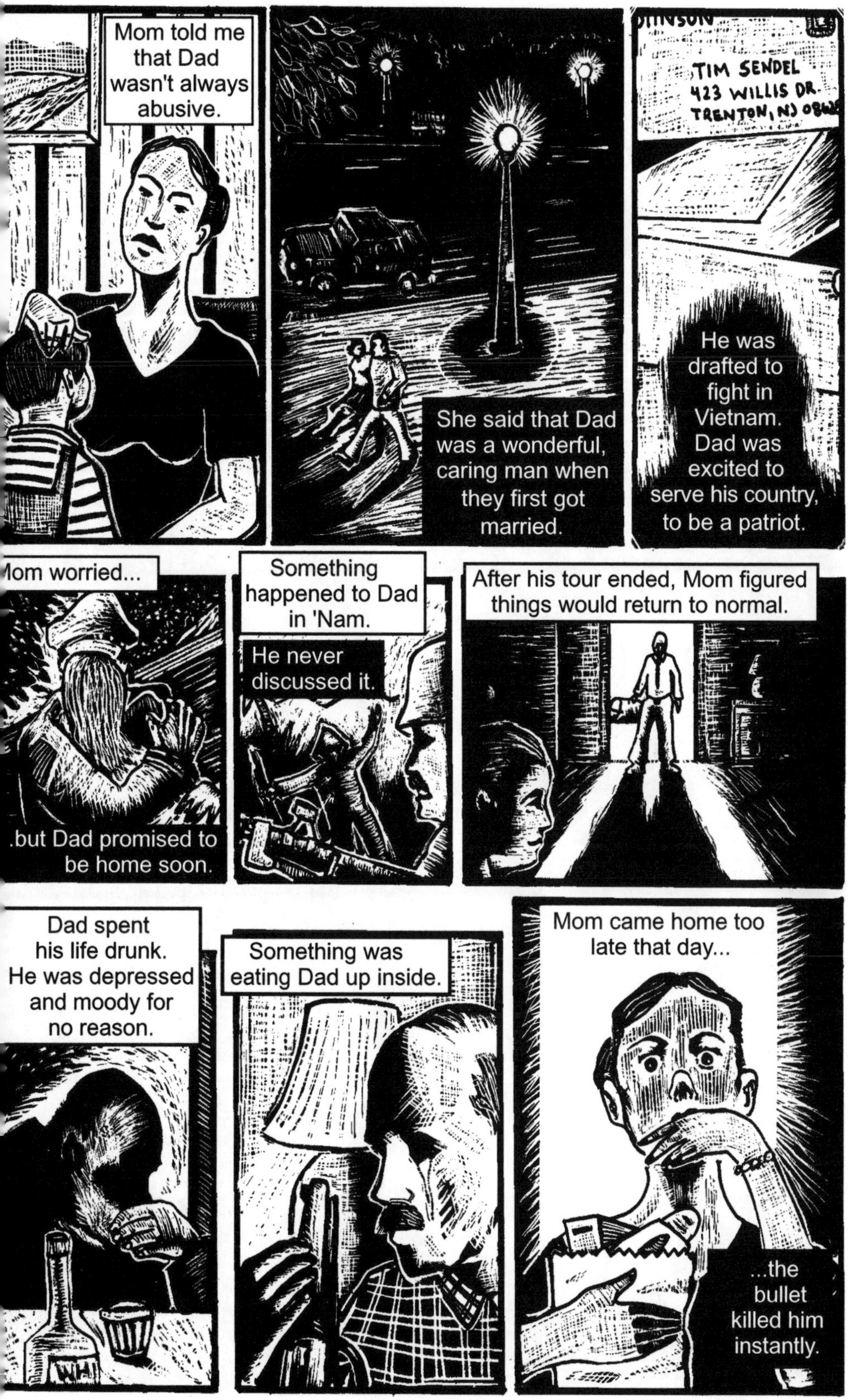

Mom told me that Dad wasn't always abusive.
She said that Dad was a wonderful, caring man when they first got married.
TIM SENDEL
423 WILLIS DR.
TRENTON, NJ
He was drafted to fight in Vietnam. Dad was excited to serve his country, to be a patriot.
Mom worried...
...but Dad promised to be home soon.
Something happened to Dad in 'Nam.
He never discussed it.
After his tour ended, Mom figured things would return to normal.
Dad spent his life drunk. He was depressed and moody for no reason.
Something was eating Dad up inside.
Mom came home too late that day...
...the bullet killed him instantly.

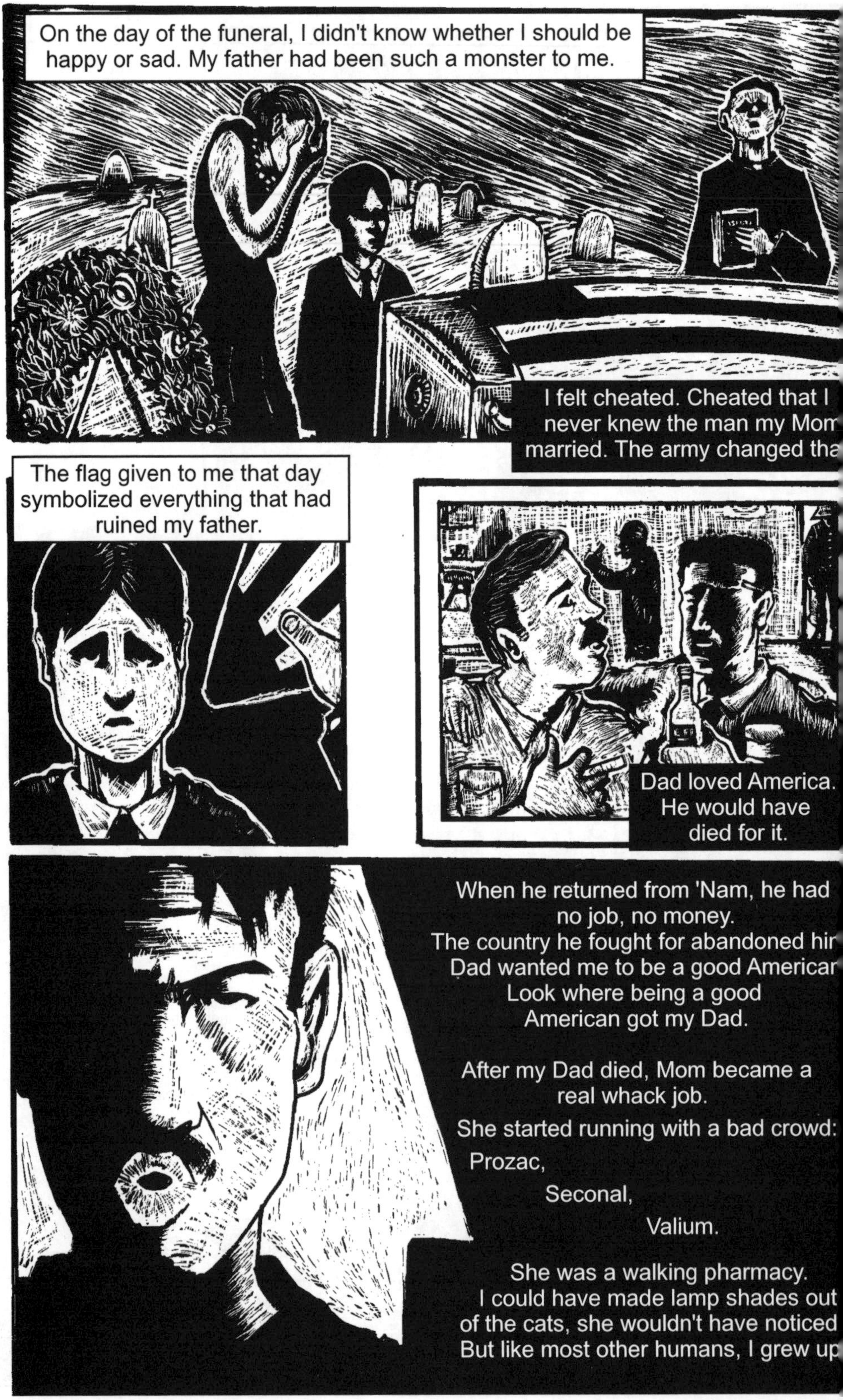

On the day of the funeral, I didn't know whether I should be happy or sad. My father had been such a monster to me.
I felt cheated. Cheated that I never knew the man my Mom married. The army changed tha
The flag given to me that day symbolized everything that had ruined my father.
Dad loved America. He would have died for it.
When he returned from 'Nam, he had no job, no money.
The country he fought for abandoned hi
Dad wanted me to be a good America
Look where being a good American got my Dad.
After my Dad died, Mom became a real whack job.
She started running with a bad crowd:
Prozac,
Seconal,
Valium.
She was a walking pharmacy.
I could have made lamp shades out of the cats, she wouldn't have noticed
But like most other humans, I grew up

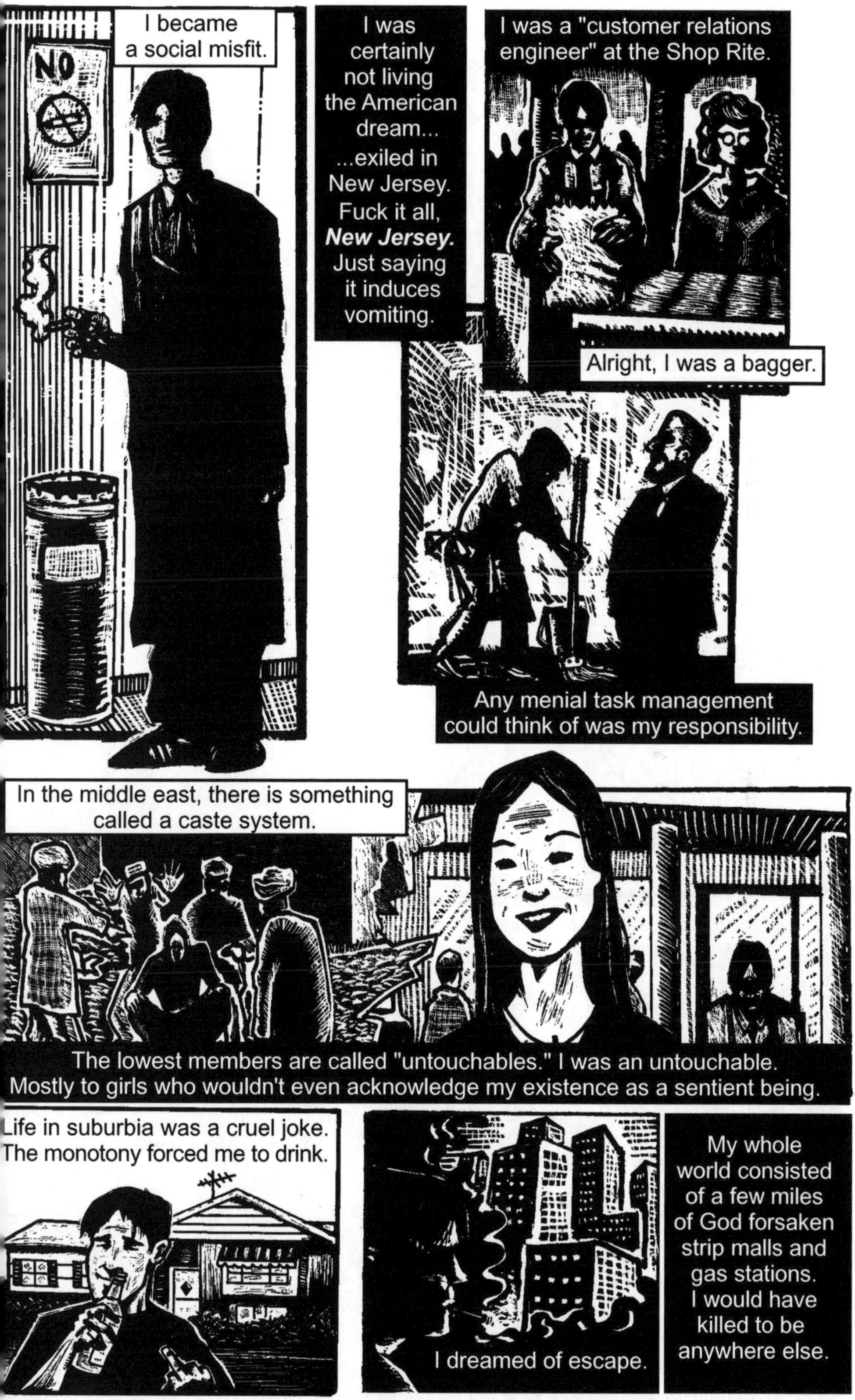

I became a social misfit.
NO
I was certainly not living the American dream... ...exiled in New Jersey. Fuck it all, ***New Jersey.*** Just saying it induces vomiting.
I was a "customer relations engineer" at the Shop Rite.
Alright, I was a bagger.
Any menial task management could think of was my responsibility.
In the middle east, there is something called a caste system.
The lowest members are called "untouchables." I was an untouchable. Mostly to girls who wouldn't even acknowledge my existence as a sentient being.
Life in suburbia was a cruel joke. The monotony forced me to drink.
I dreamed of escape.
My whole world consisted of a few miles of God forsaken strip malls and gas stations. I would have killed to be anywhere else.

Like most other 16 year olds, I attended high school...

...occasionally.

I was routinely harassed by every subnormal and delinquent who dragged their knuckles through the hallowed halls of my dilapidated public learning institution. Needless to say, it was not the most conducive educational environment.

The blacks routinely beat me because I wasn't black.

The rich white jocks beat me...

...because I wasn't rich and I wasn't a jock

It wasn't that I didn't like the nerds...

$\frac{2(3m/8)}{7s} = T$

$8(7.1Y) + .903 \frac{(78.96)}{-Y/3.14} = T$

...I just couldn't understand them.

The few friends I had were just like me...

disturbed.

Our bible was a bunch of print outs I made from the internet called "The Jolly Roger."

Daily, we would ponder its teachings.

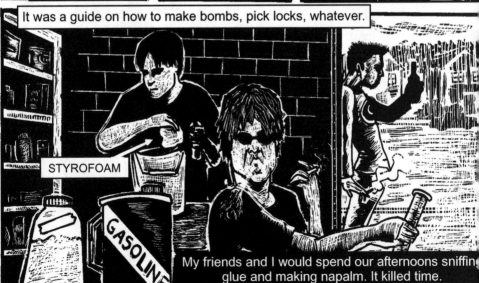

It was a guide on how to make bombs, pick locks, whatever.

STYROFOAM

GASOLINE

My friends and I would spend our afternoons sniffing glue and making napalm. It killed time.

They say idle hands do the devil's work...

...my friends and I certainly proved that axiom correct.

Sure we blew things up and huffed paint thinner fumes, why not? At that point in my my life, I had no concept of a greater good. No religious beliefs. If you had asked me what the Koran was, I probably would have replied a character on *Star Trek*.

And then I met Salim.

He was a new employee at the market where I worked. A cagey, Pakistani guy.

Salim owned a small market of his own.

He would steal food from our market and resell it at his.

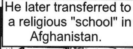

Scamming the customers...

...or skimming from the registers...

...Salim always had an angle.

It's no surprise that we quickly became friends.

Salim had studied political science in Karachi...

He later transferred to a religious "school" in Afghanistan.

¡PELIGRO!

Salim was always eager to share his knowledge with me.

It certainly made the time pass faster.

One night, after inhaling a bunch of Whip-Its in the dairy section, I stumbled outside to find Salim.

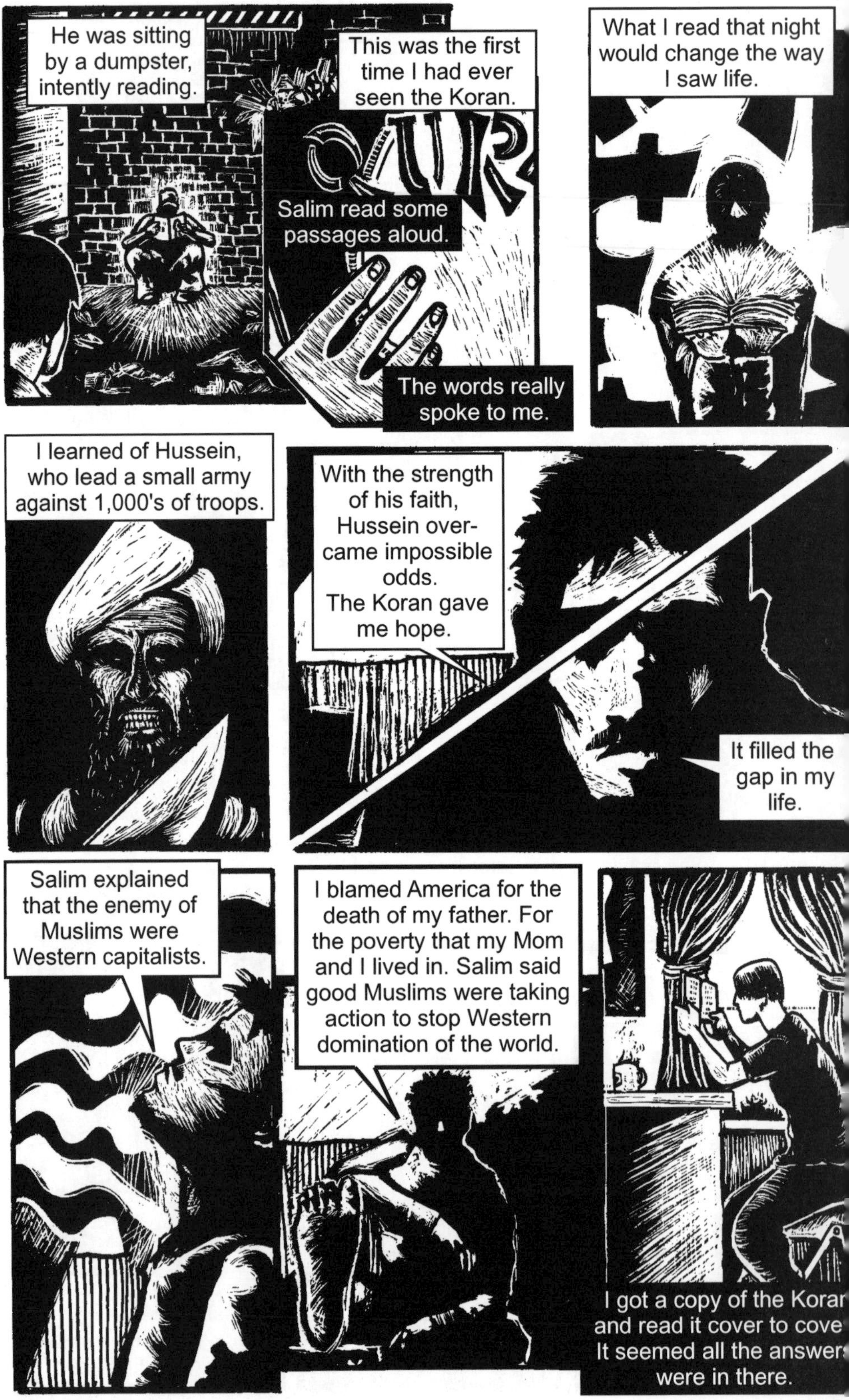
He was sitting by a dumpster, intently reading.
This was the first time I had ever seen the Koran.
Salim read some passages aloud.
The words really spoke to me.
What I read that night would change the way I saw life.
I learned of Hussein, who lead a small army against 1,000's of troops.
With the strength of his faith, Hussein over-came impossible odds. The Koran gave me hope.
It filled the gap in my life.
Salim explained that the enemy of Muslims were Western capitalists.
I blamed America for the death of my father. For the poverty that my Mom and I lived in. Salim said good Muslims were taking action to stop Western domination of the world.
I got a copy of the Koran and read it cover to cove It seemed all the answer were in there.

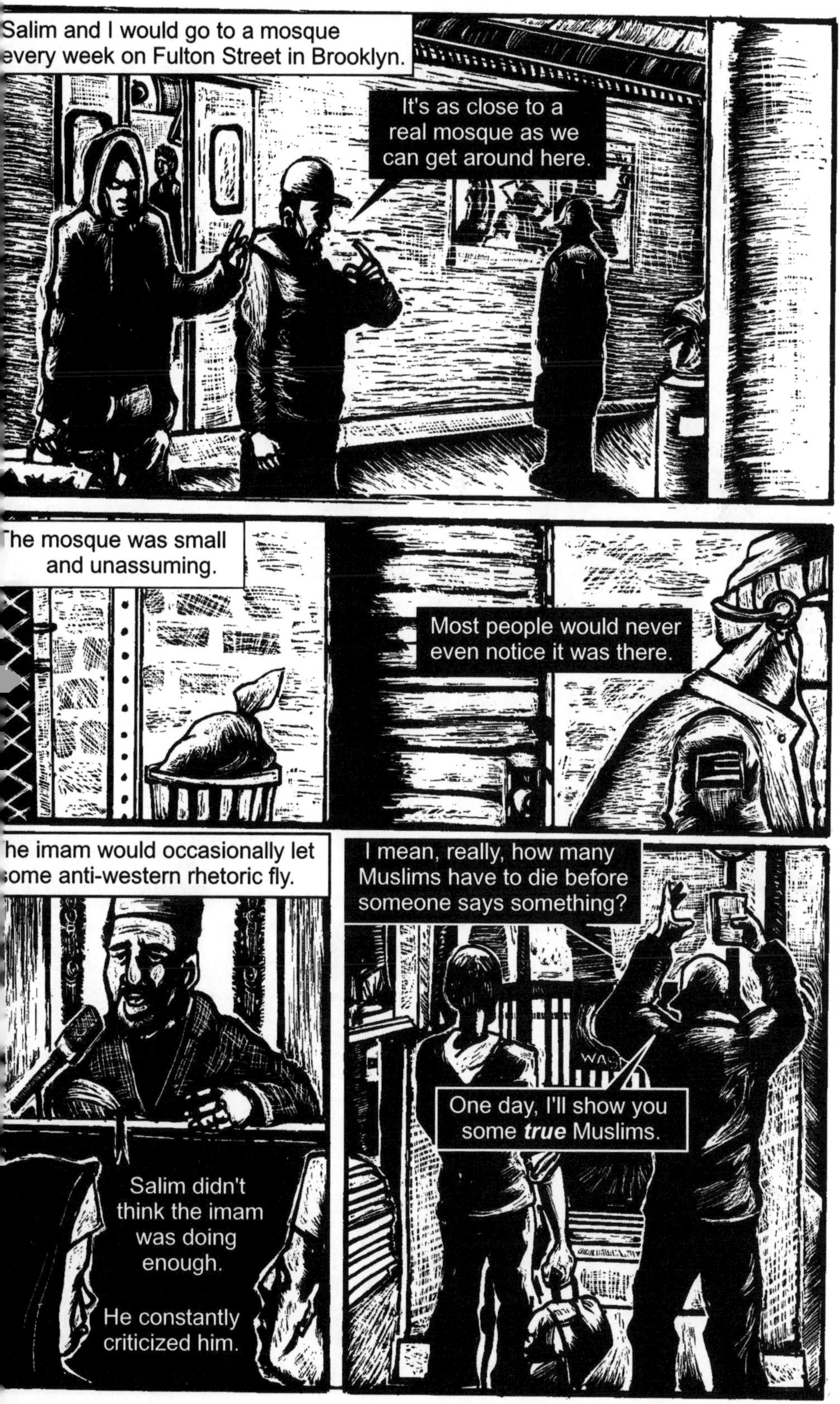

Salim and I would go to a mosque every week on Fulton Street in Brooklyn.
It's as close to a real mosque as we can get around here.
The mosque was small and unassuming.
Most people would never even notice it was there.
The imam would occasionally let some anti-western rhetoric fly.
Salim didn't think the imam was doing enough.
He constantly criticized him.
I mean, really, how many Muslims have to die before someone says something?
One day, I'll show you some *true* Muslims.

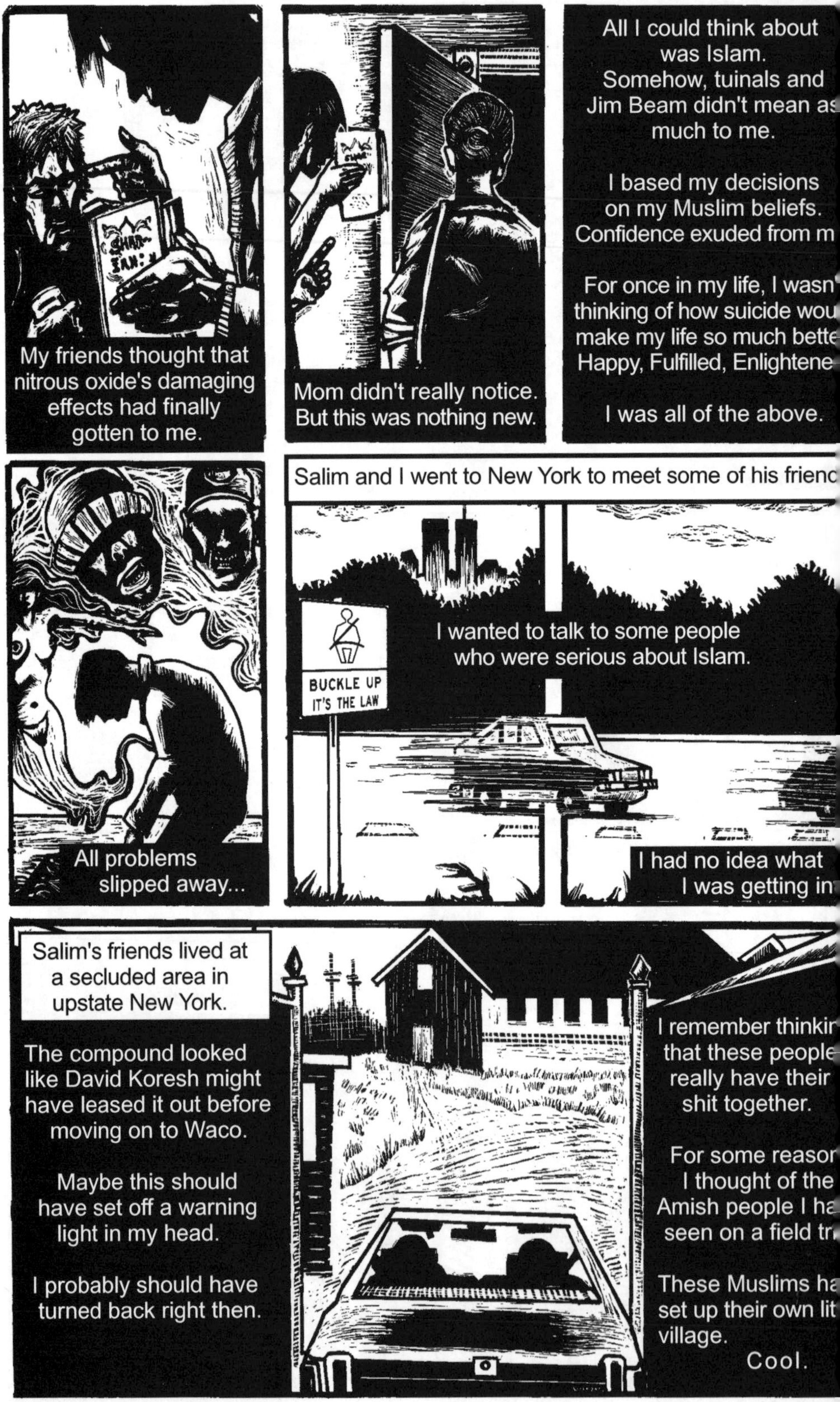
My friends thought that nitrous oxide's damaging effects had finally gotten to me.
Mom didn't really notice. But this was nothing new.
All I could think about was Islam.
Somehow, tuinals and Jim Beam didn't mean as much to me.
I based my decisions on my Muslim beliefs.
Confidence exuded from m
For once in my life, I wasn
thinking of how suicide wou
make my life so much bette
Happy, Fulfilled, Enlightene
I was all of the above.
All problems slipped away...
Salim and I went to New York to meet some of his frienc
BUCKLE UP IT'S THE LAW
I wanted to talk to some people who were serious about Islam.
I had no idea what I was getting in
Salim's friends lived at a secluded area in upstate New York.
The compound looked like David Koresh might have leased it out before moving on to Waco.
Maybe this should have set off a warning light in my head.
I probably should have turned back right then.
I remember thinkir
that these people
really have their
shit together.
For some reasor
I thought of the
Amish people I ha
seen on a field tr
These Muslims ha
set up their own lit
village.
Cool.

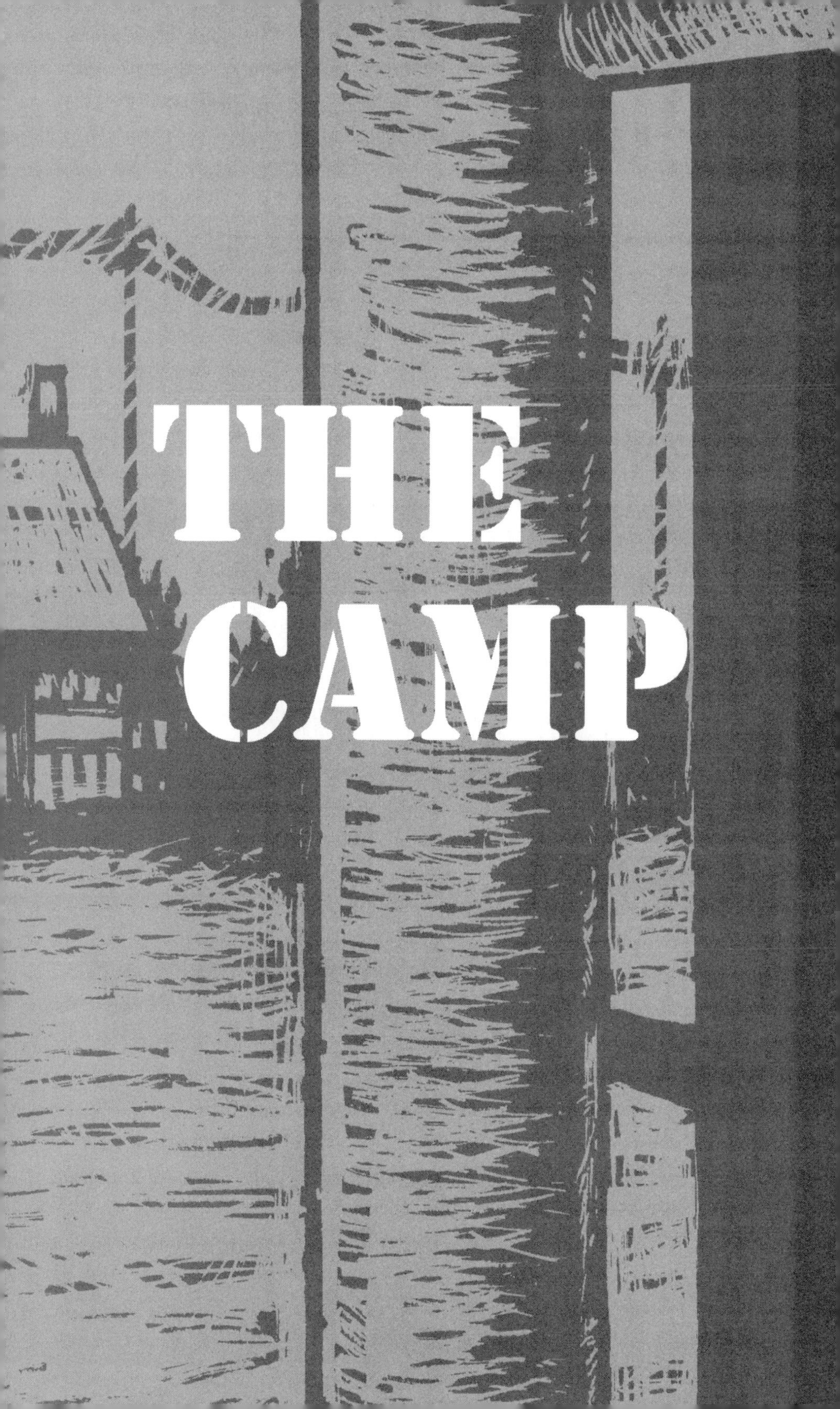

THE CAMP

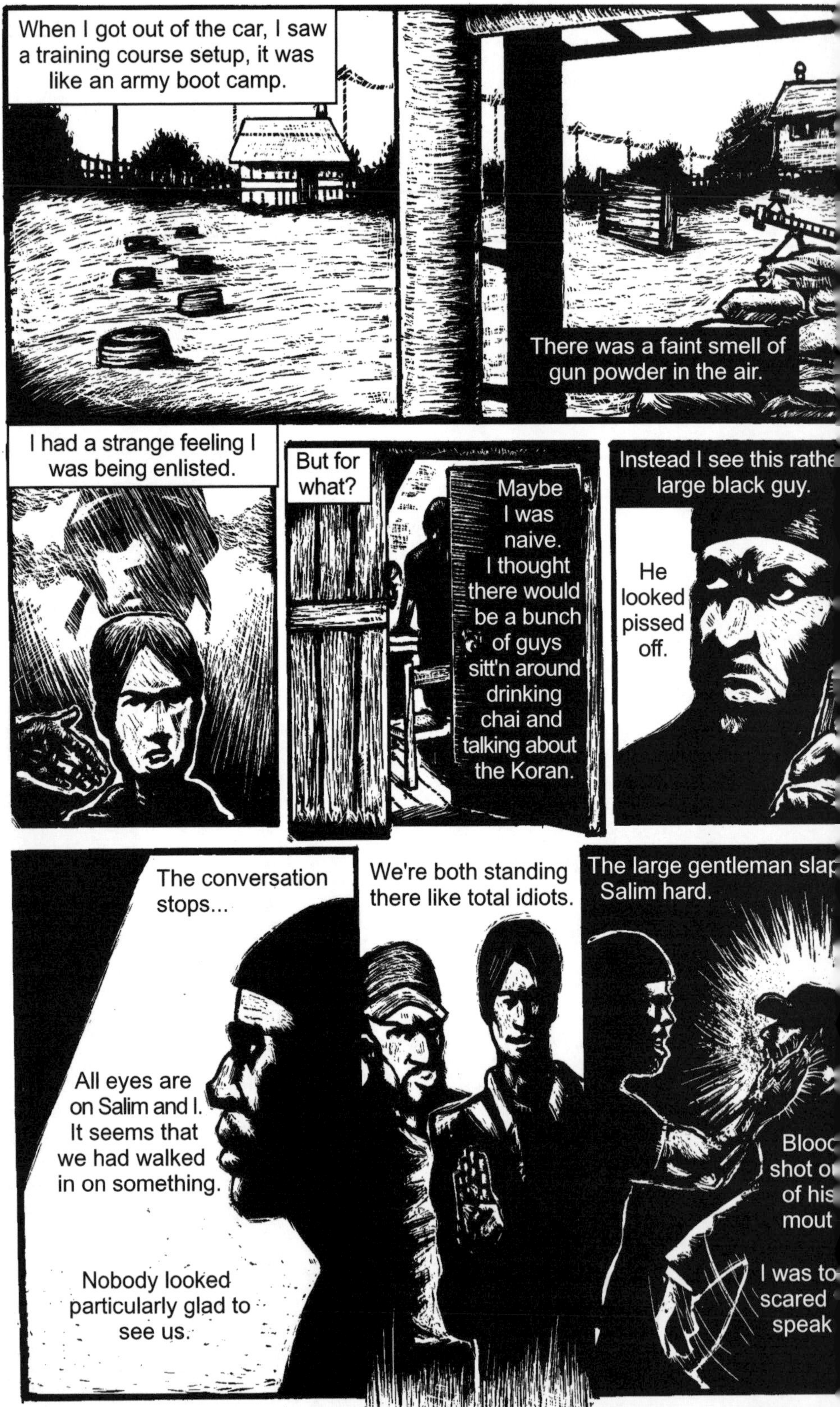

When I got out of the car, I saw a training course setup, it was like an army boot camp.
There was a faint smell of gun powder in the air.
I had a strange feeling I was being enlisted.
But for what?
Maybe I was naive. I thought there would be a bunch of guys sitt'n around drinking chai and talking about the Koran.
Instead I see this rathe large black guy.
He looked pissed off.
The conversation stops...
All eyes are on Salim and I. It seems that we had walked in on something.
Nobody looked particularly glad to see us.
We're both standing there like total idiots.
The large gentleman slap Salim hard.
Blooc shot o of his mout
I was to scared speak

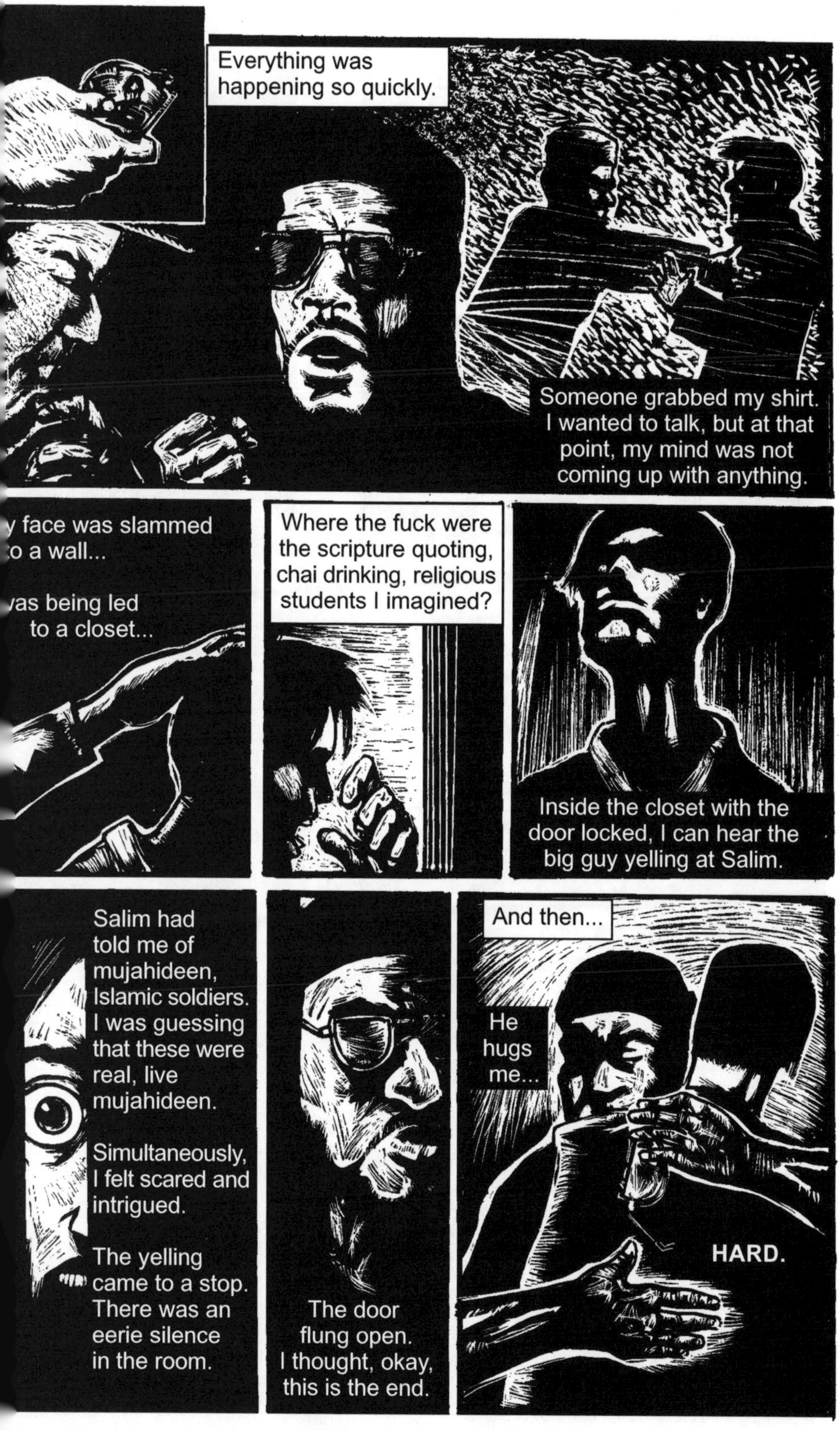
Everything was happening so quickly.
Someone grabbed my shirt. I wanted to talk, but at that point, my mind was not coming up with anything.
face was slammed
o a wall...
as being led
to a closet...
Where the fuck were the scripture quoting, chai drinking, religious students I imagined?
Inside the closet with the door locked, I can hear the big guy yelling at Salim.
Salim had told me of mujahideen, Islamic soldiers. I was guessing that these were real, live mujahideen.
Simultaneously, I felt scared and intrigued.
The yelling came to a stop. There was an eerie silence in the room.
The door flung open. I thought, okay, this is the end.
And then...
He hugs me...
HARD.

I was utterly confused.

Salim was in the corner looking dejected.

Everyone in the room had smiles on their faces.

Even the brute that shoved me in the close

I am truly sorry, little brother. My name is Kazeem. Welcome. Salim did not mention you were...

white.

That's how I met Kazeer

You see, we must be careful. There are those who would like to stop our operation.

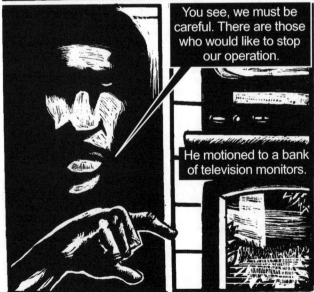

He motioned to a bank of television monitors.

A very suspicious looking white van was on the TV.

We watch them as they watch us.

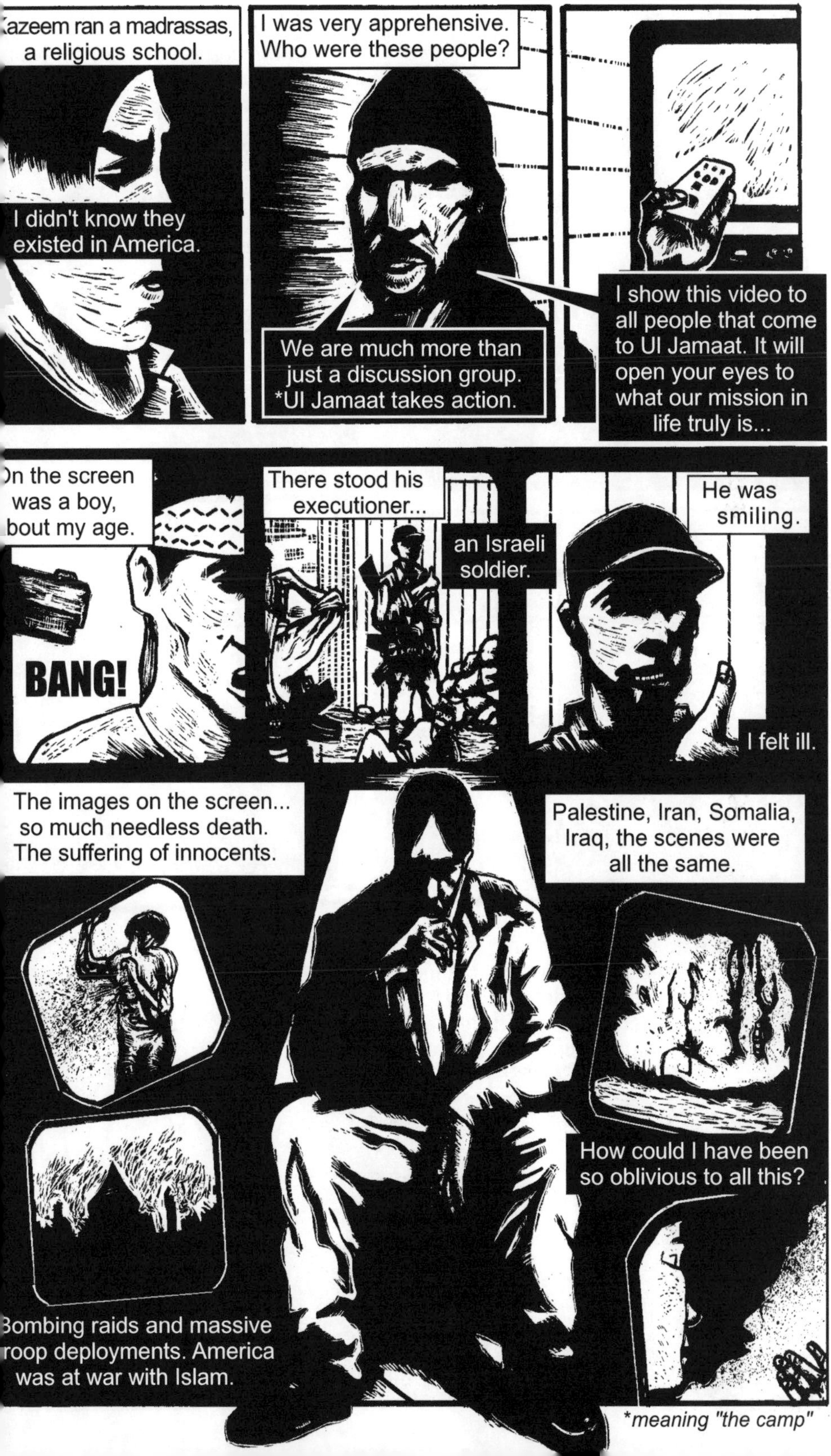
azeem ran a madrassas, a religious school.
I didn't know they existed in America.
I was very apprehensive. Who were these people?
We are much more than just a discussion group. *Ul Jamaat takes action.
I show this video to all people that come to Ul Jamaat. It will open your eyes to what our mission in life truly is...
n the screen was a boy, bout my age.
BANG!
There stood his executioner...
an Israeli soldier.
He was smiling.
I felt ill.
The images on the screen... so much needless death. The suffering of innocents.
Palestine, Iran, Somalia, Iraq, the scenes were all the same.
How could I have been so oblivious to all this?
ombing raids and massive roop deployments. America was at war with Islam.

*meaning "the camp"

My mind was racing. Kazeem told me to get some rest and ponder what I had seen. The next day, I would see the operation.

Kazeem wanted me to join up. After that video, I felt it was my moral duty to join.

Yeah, I had inexplicably developed morals.

The next morning, the previously barren camp was teeming with people. I noticed quite a few had gu

In another section of the camp was a shooting range. Men shot M-16's at silhouetted targets, riddling them with bulle

If the targets were real men, there would be extensive lacerations, large central holes with scalloped margins, but most likely a smaller central defect since the distance and bullet caliber (in this case a 5.56mm ammunition) factor heavily.

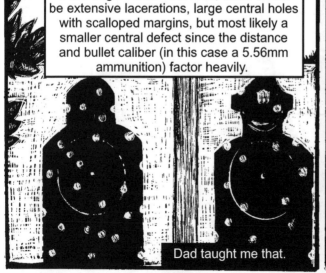

Dad taught me that.

ZIONIS PIG!

There was little doubt th these guys were seriou

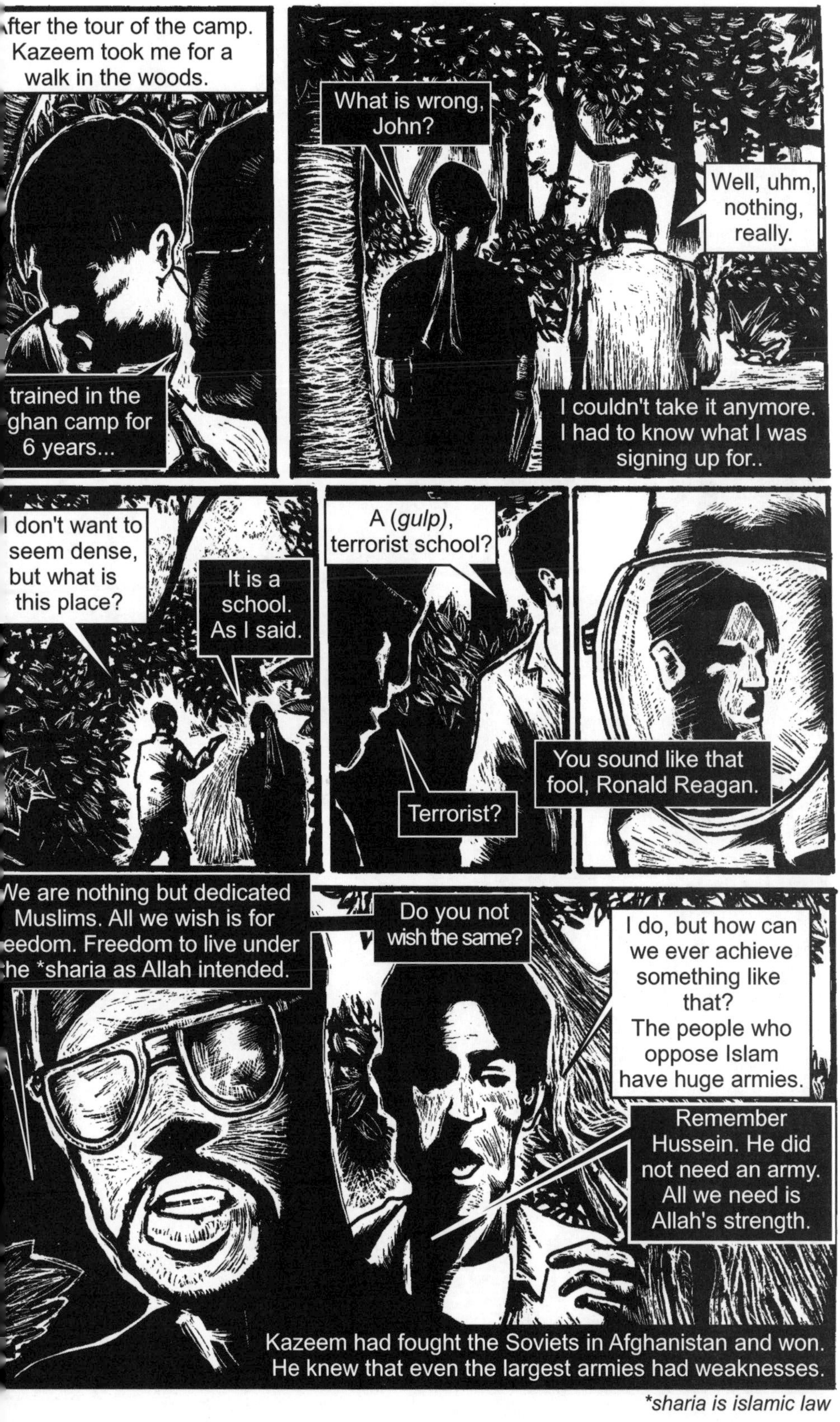
fter the tour of the camp. Kazeem took me for a walk in the woods.
trained in the ghan camp for 6 years...
What is wrong, John?
Well, uhm, nothing, really.
I couldn't take it anymore. I had to know what I was signing up for..
I don't want to seem dense, but what is this place?
It is a school. As I said.
A (gulp), terrorist school?
Terrorist?
You sound like that fool, Ronald Reagan.
We are nothing but dedicated Muslims. All we wish is for eedom. Freedom to live under he *sharia as Allah intended.
Do you not wish the same?
I do, but how can we ever achieve something like that? The people who oppose Islam have huge armies.
Remember Hussein. He did not need an army. All we need is Allah's strength.
Kazeem had fought the Soviets in Afghanistan and won. He knew that even the largest armies had weaknesses.

**sharia is islamic law*

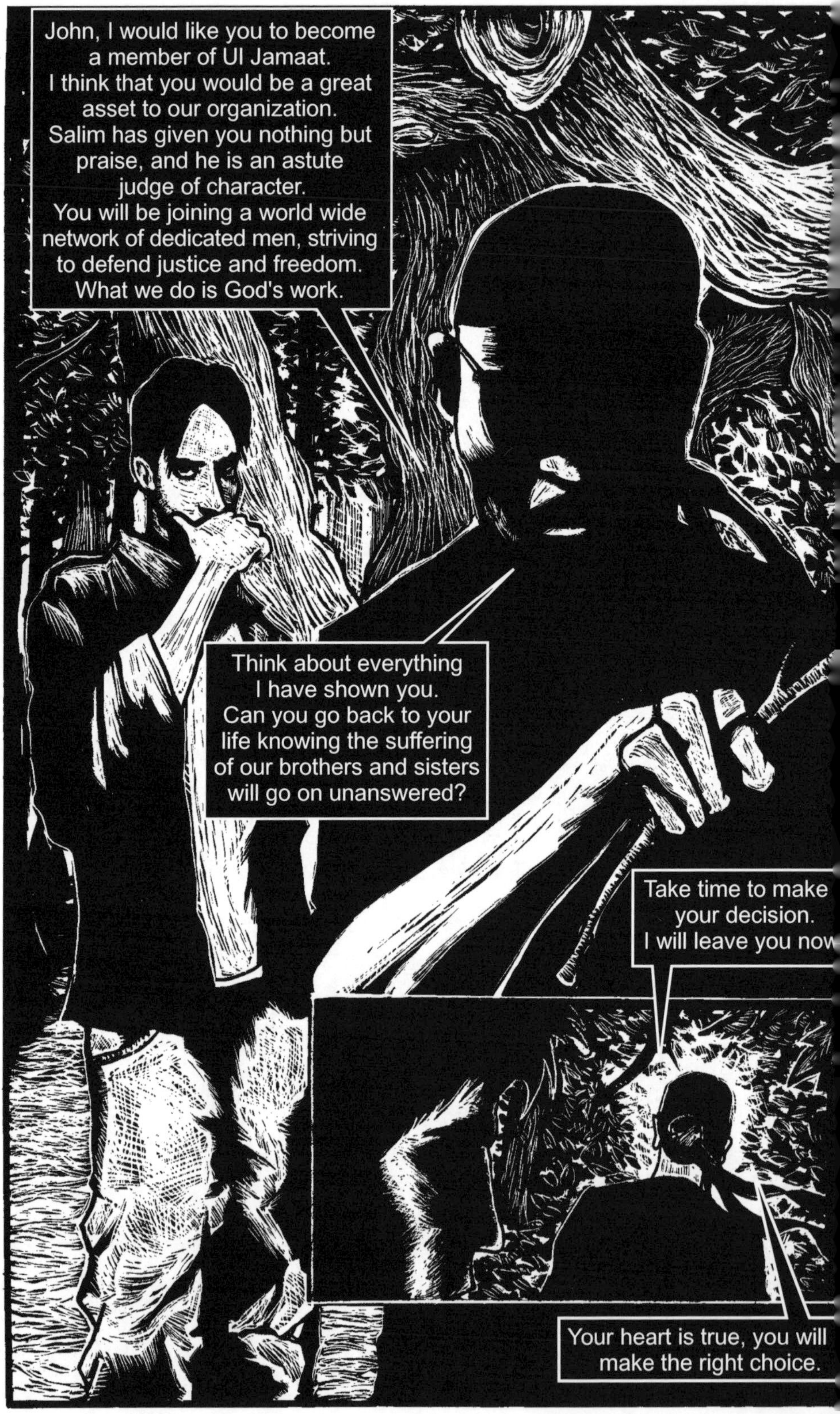
John, I would like you to become a member of Ul Jamaat. I think that you would be a great asset to our organization. Salim has given you nothing but praise, and he is an astute judge of character. You will be joining a world wide network of dedicated men, striving to defend justice and freedom. What we do is God's work.
Think about everything I have shown you. Can you go back to your life knowing the suffering of our brothers and sisters will go on unanswered?
Take time to make your decision. I will leave you now
Your heart is true, you will make the right choice.

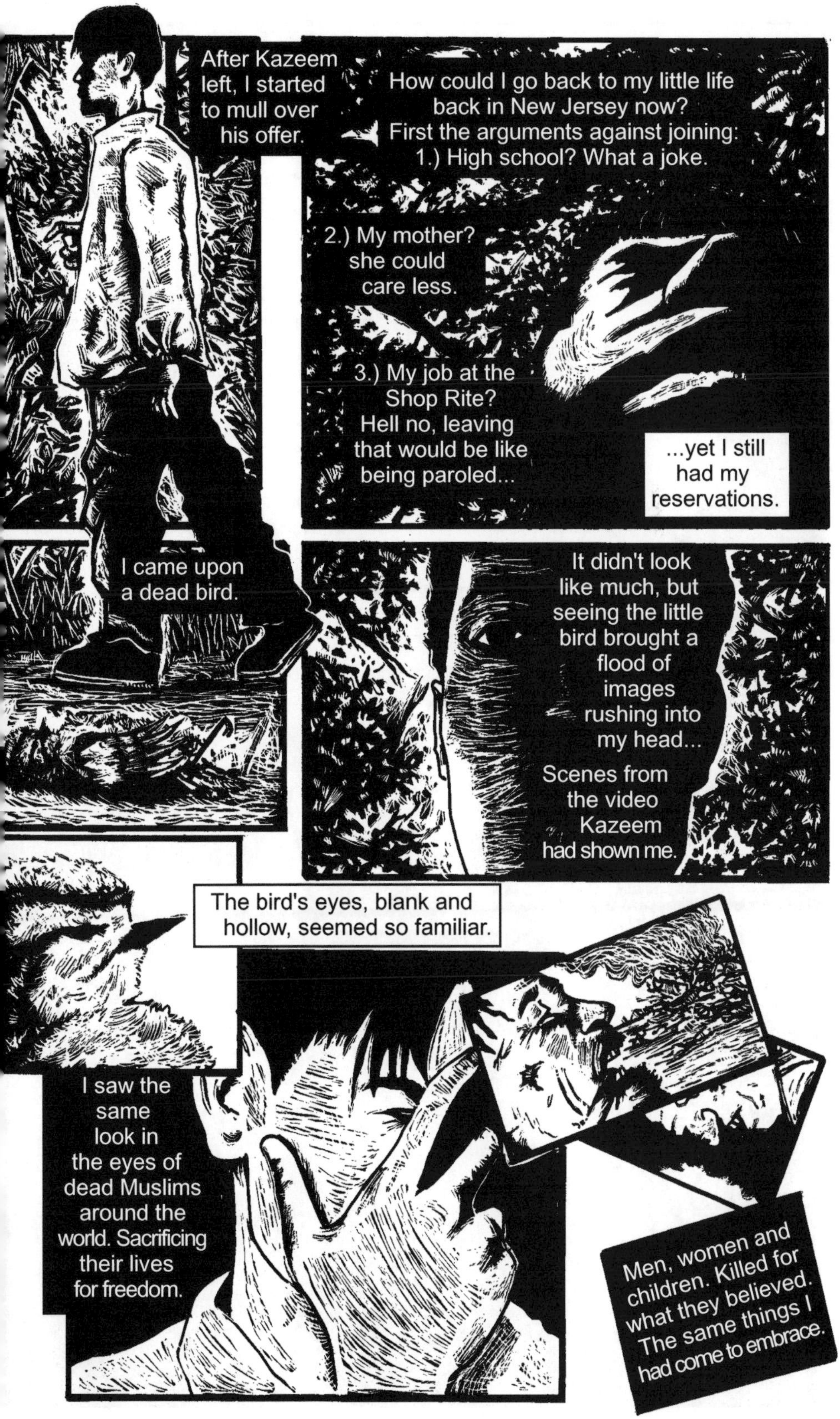

After Kazeem left, I started to mull over his offer.
How could I go back to my little life back in New Jersey now? First the arguments against joining: 1.) High school? What a joke.
2.) My mother? she could care less.
3.) My job at the Shop Rite? Hell no, leaving that would be like being paroled...
...yet I still had my reservations.
I came upon a dead bird.
It didn't look like much, but seeing the little bird brought a flood of images rushing into my head...
Scenes from the video Kazeem had shown me.
The bird's eyes, blank and hollow, seemed so familiar.
I saw the same look in the eyes of dead Muslims around the world. Sacrificing their lives for freedom.
Men, women and children. Killed for what they believed. The same things I had come to embrace.

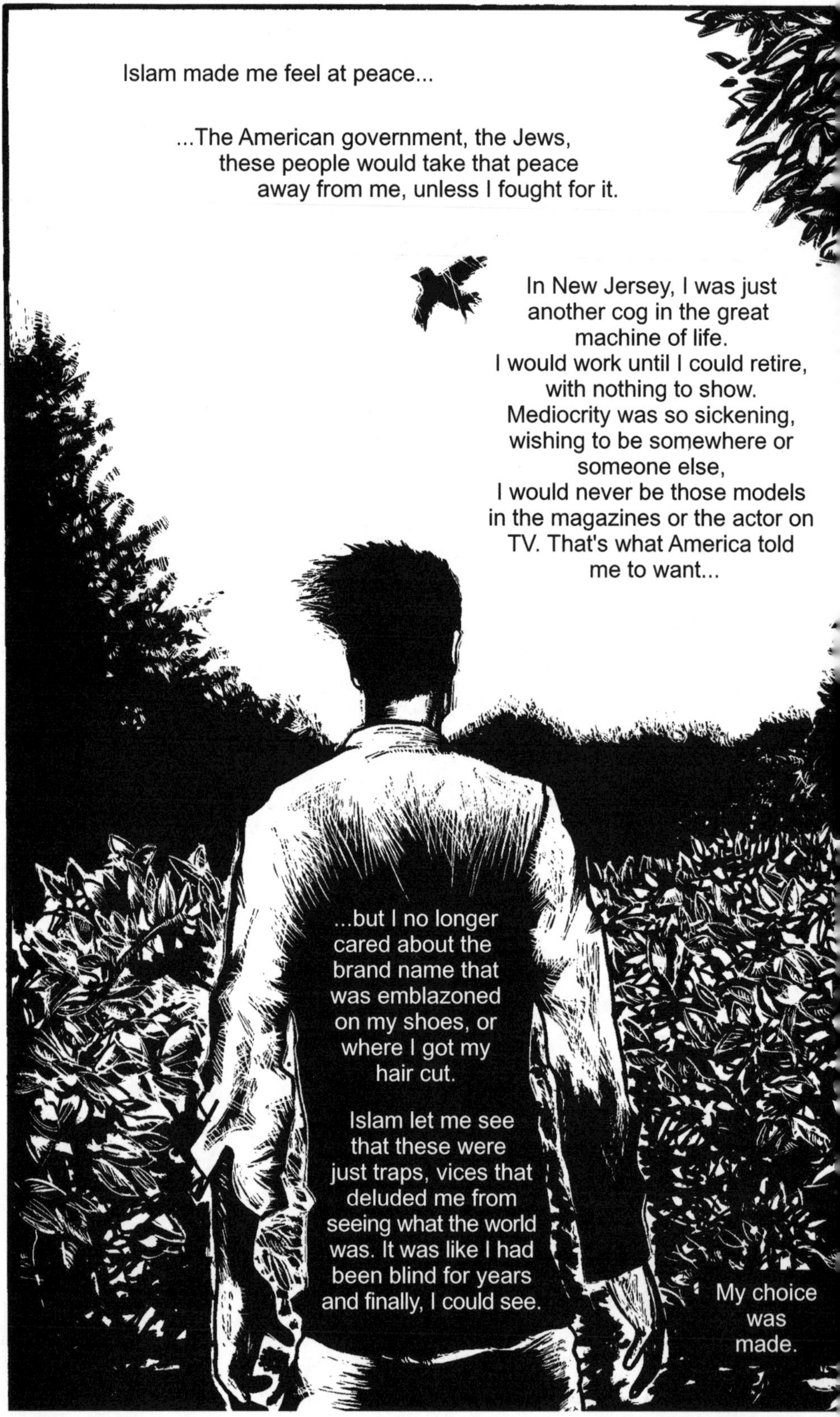

Islam made me feel at peace...
...The American government, the Jews, these people would take that peace away from me, unless I fought for it.
In New Jersey, I was just another cog in the great machine of life. I would work until I could retire, with nothing to show. Mediocrity was so sickening, wishing to be somewhere or someone else, I would never be those models in the magazines or the actor on TV. That's what America told me to want...
...but I no longer cared about the brand name that was emblazoned on my shoes, or where I got my hair cut.
Islam let me see that these were just traps, vices that deluded me from seeing what the world was. It was like I had been blind for years and finally, I could see.
My choice was made.

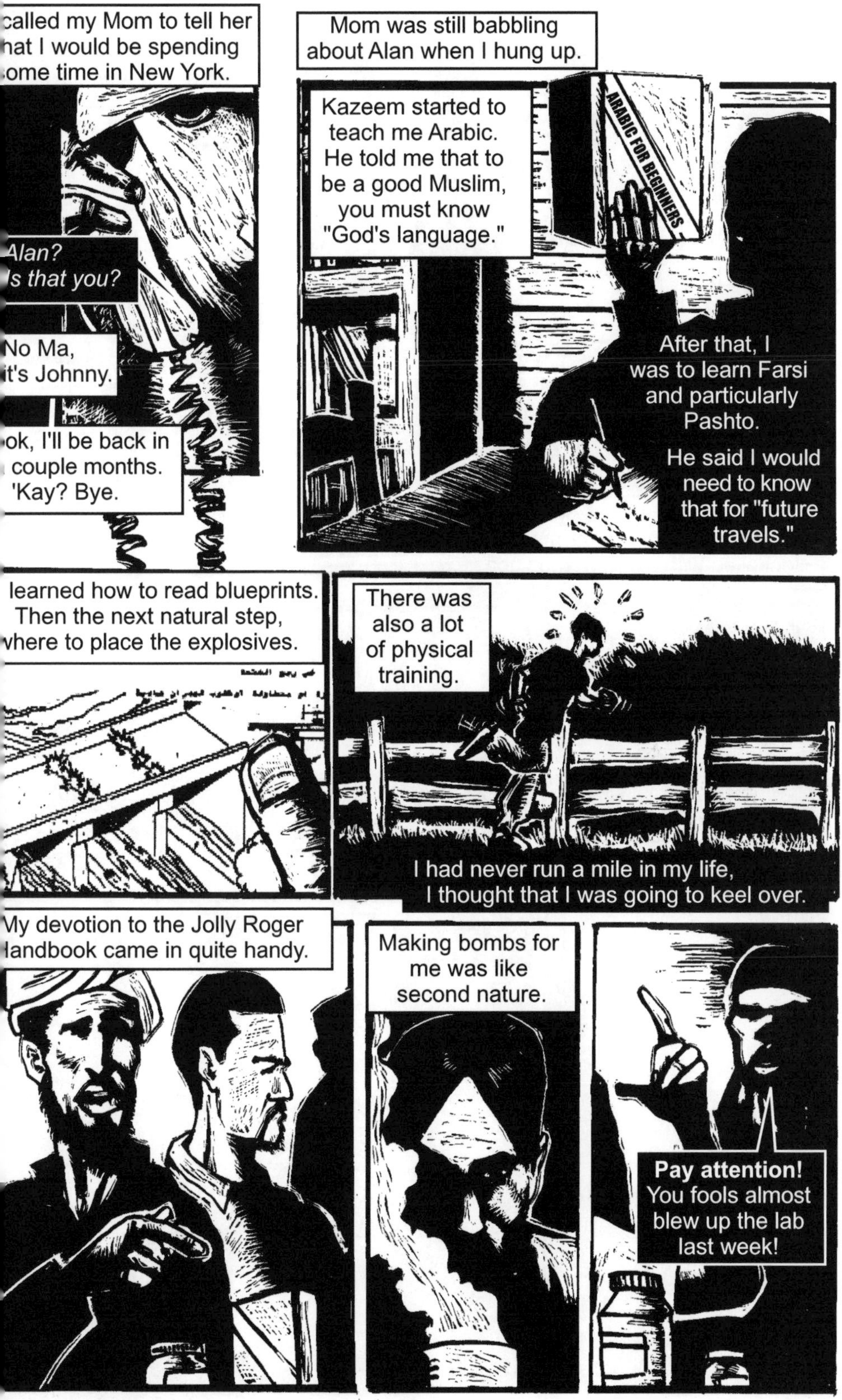

called my Mom to tell her
hat I would be spending
ome time in New York.
Alan?
Is that you?
No Ma,
it's Johnny.
ok, I'll be back in
couple months.
'Kay? Bye.
Mom was still babbling
about Alan when I hung up.
Kazeem started to
teach me Arabic.
He told me that to
be a good Muslim,
you must know
"God's language."
ARABIC FOR BEGINNERS
After that, I
was to learn Farsi
and particularly
Pashto.
He said I would
need to know
that for "future
travels."
learned how to read blueprints.
Then the next natural step,
vhere to place the explosives.
There was
also a lot
of physical
training.
I had never run a mile in my life,
I thought that I was going to keel over.
My devotion to the Jolly Roger
Handbook came in quite handy.
Making bombs for
me was like
second nature.
Pay attention!
You fools almost
blew up the lab
last week!

I would go to the local hard-ware store to purchase materials to make bombs.

Rocket engine powder is great 'cause you can use it as is. It's easy to get (for model rockets). I suggest the 2-T size for the D engine rocket...

Flash Powder, fertilizer, whatever. I had to get rocket engine powder at the hobby shop.

It's the most potent grade. And at $5.00 a packet, a genuine b

There was also military weaponry at the camp. Storage rooms were stockpiled with different munitions.

Kazeem knew a grunt tha would lift stuff from the arm base at Fort Dix and resell

I was given a thick stack of photocopies which broke down how to be a terrorist.

Encyclopedia
of
Jihad

It was pretty comprehensive.

From evading cops to making bombs out of wristwatches, it was all there.

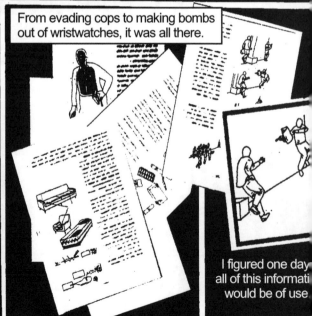

I figured one day all of this informati would be of use

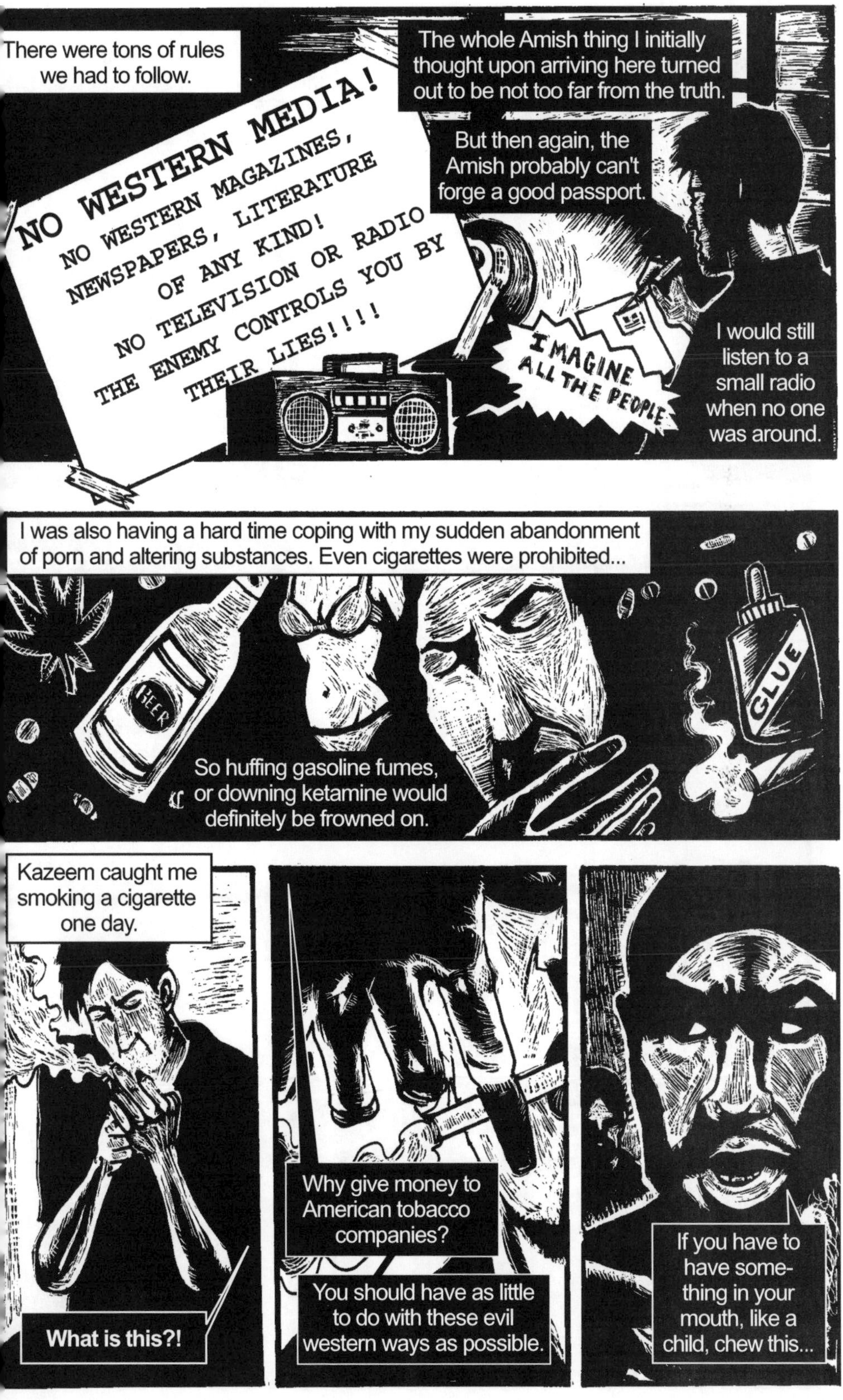
There were tons of rules we had to follow.
NO WESTERN MEDIA!
NO WESTERN MAGAZINES, NEWSPAPERS, LITERATURE OF ANY KIND!
NO TELEVISION OR RADIO
THE ENEMY CONTROLS YOU BY THEIR LIES!!!!
The whole Amish thing I initially thought upon arriving here turned out to be not too far from the truth.
But then again, the Amish probably can't forge a good passport.
IMAGINE ALL THE PEOPLE
I would still listen to a small radio when no one was around.
I was also having a hard time coping with my sudden abandonment of porn and altering substances. Even cigarettes were prohibited...
BEER
GLUE
So huffing gasoline fumes, or downing ketamine would definitely be frowned on.
Kazeem caught me smoking a cigarette one day.
What is this?!
Why give money to American tobacco companies?
You should have as little to do with these evil western ways as possible.
If you have to have something in your mouth, like a child, chew this...

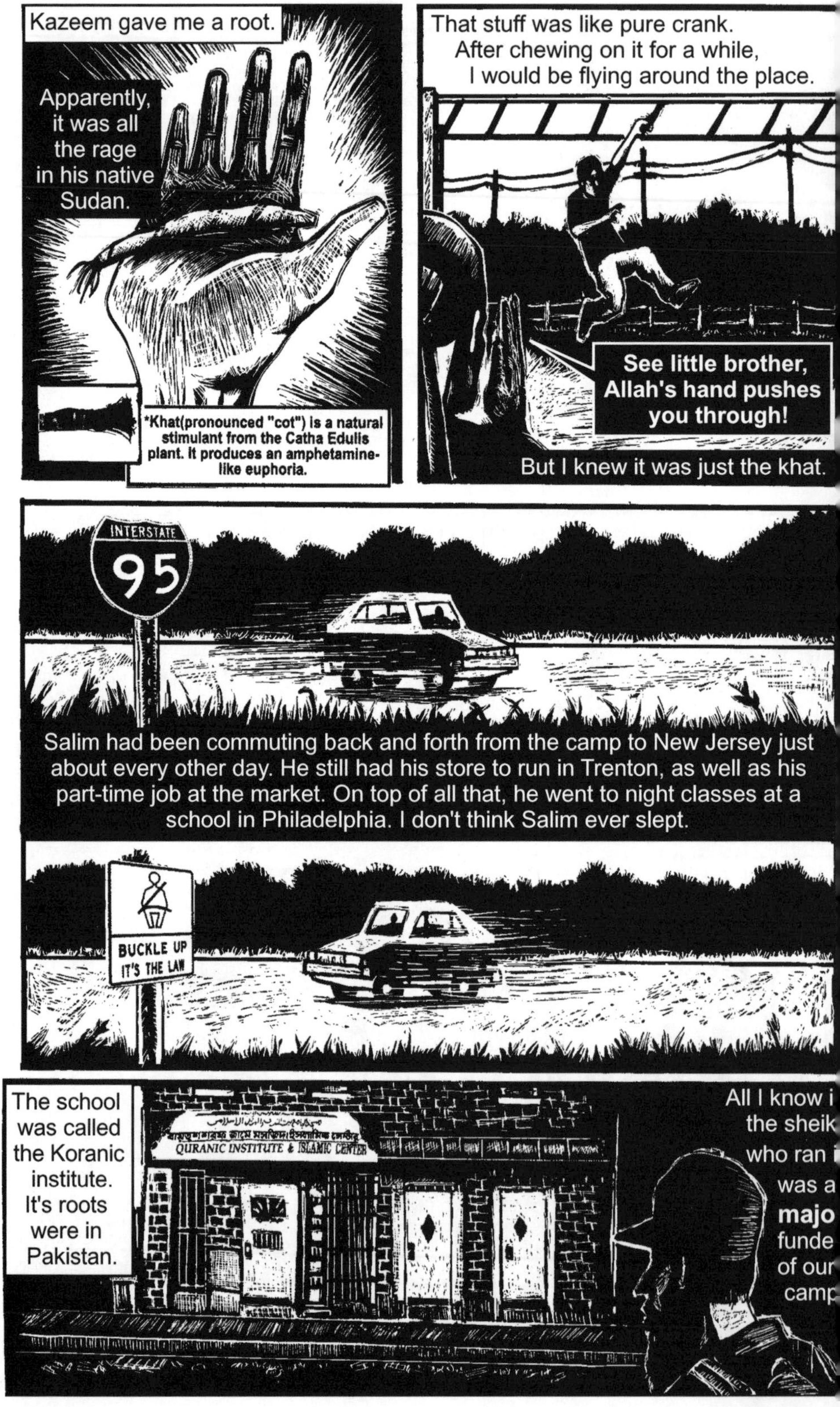
Kazeem gave me a root.
Apparently, it was all the rage in his native Sudan.
*Khat(pronounced "cot") is a natural stimulant from the Catha Edulis plant. It produces an amphetamine-like euphoria.
That stuff was like pure crank. After chewing on it for a while, I would be flying around the place.
See little brother, Allah's hand pushes you through!
But I knew it was just the khat.
INTERSTATE
95
Salim had been commuting back and forth from the camp to New Jersey just about every other day. He still had his store to run in Trenton, as well as his part-time job at the market. On top of all that, he went to night classes at a school in Philadelphia. I don't think Salim ever slept.
BUCKLE UP
IT'S THE LAW
The school was called the Koranic institute. It's roots were in Pakistan.
QURANIC INSTITUTE & ISLAMIC CENTER
All I know i
the sheik
who ran
was a
majo
funde
of our
camp

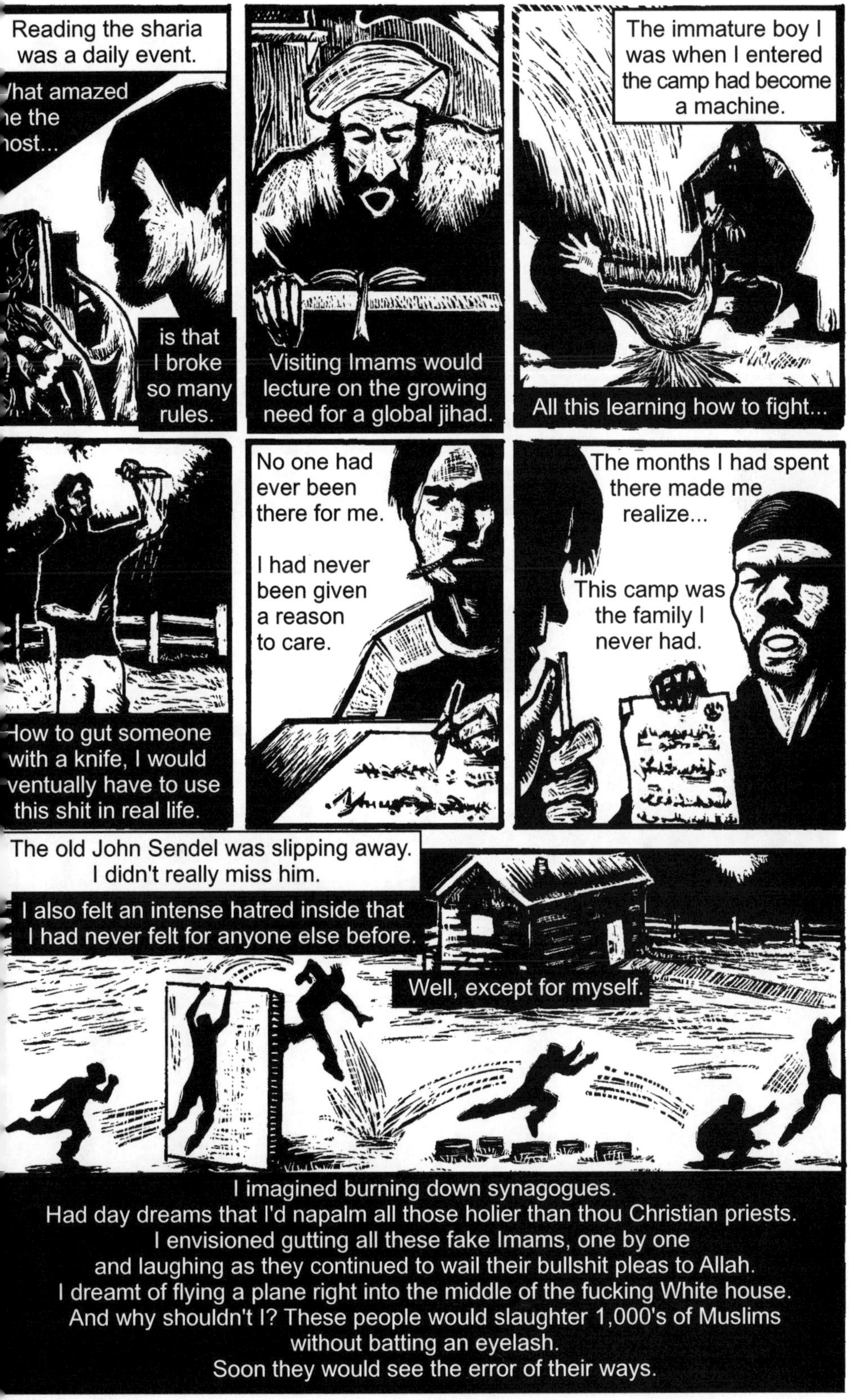
Reading the sharia was a daily event.
/hat amazed ie the iost...
is that I broke so many rules.
Visiting Imams would lecture on the growing need for a global jihad.
The immature boy I was when I entered the camp had become a machine.
All this learning how to fight...
How to gut someone with a knife, I would ventually have to use this shit in real life.
No one had ever been there for me.
I had never been given a reason to care.
The months I had spent there made me realize...
This camp was the family I never had.
The old John Sendel was slipping away. I didn't really miss him.
I also felt an intense hatred inside that I had never felt for anyone else before.
Well, except for myself.
I imagined burning down synagogues.
Had day dreams that I'd napalm all those holier than thou Christian priests.
I envisioned gutting all these fake Imams, one by one
and laughing as they continued to wail their bullshit pleas to Allah.
I dreamt of flying a plane right into the middle of the fucking White house.
And why shouldn't I? These people would slaughter 1,000's of Muslims
without batting an eyelash.
Soon they would see the error of their ways.

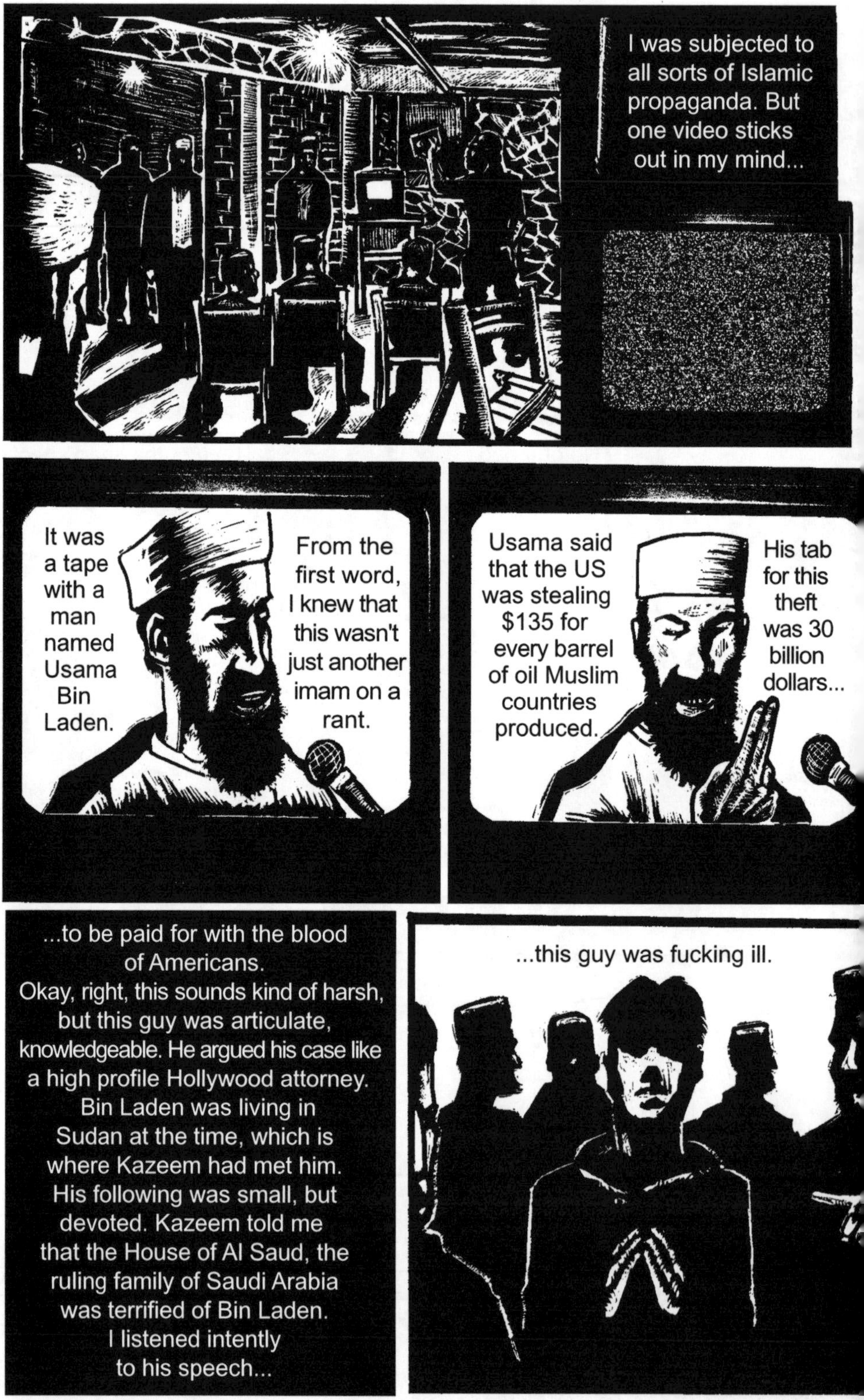
I was subjected to all sorts of Islamic propaganda. But one video sticks out in my mind...
It was a tape with a man named Usama Bin Laden.
From the first word, I knew that this wasn't just another imam on a rant.
Usama said that the US was stealing $135 for every barrel of oil Muslim countries produced.
His tab for this theft was 30 billion dollars...
...to be paid for with the blood of Americans.
Okay, right, this sounds kind of harsh, but this guy was articulate, knowledgeable. He argued his case like a high profile Hollywood attorney.
Bin Laden was living in Sudan at the time, which is where Kazeem had met him.
His following was small, but devoted. Kazeem told me that the House of Al Saud, the ruling family of Saudi Arabia was terrified of Bin Laden.
I listened intently to his speech...
...this guy was fucking ill.

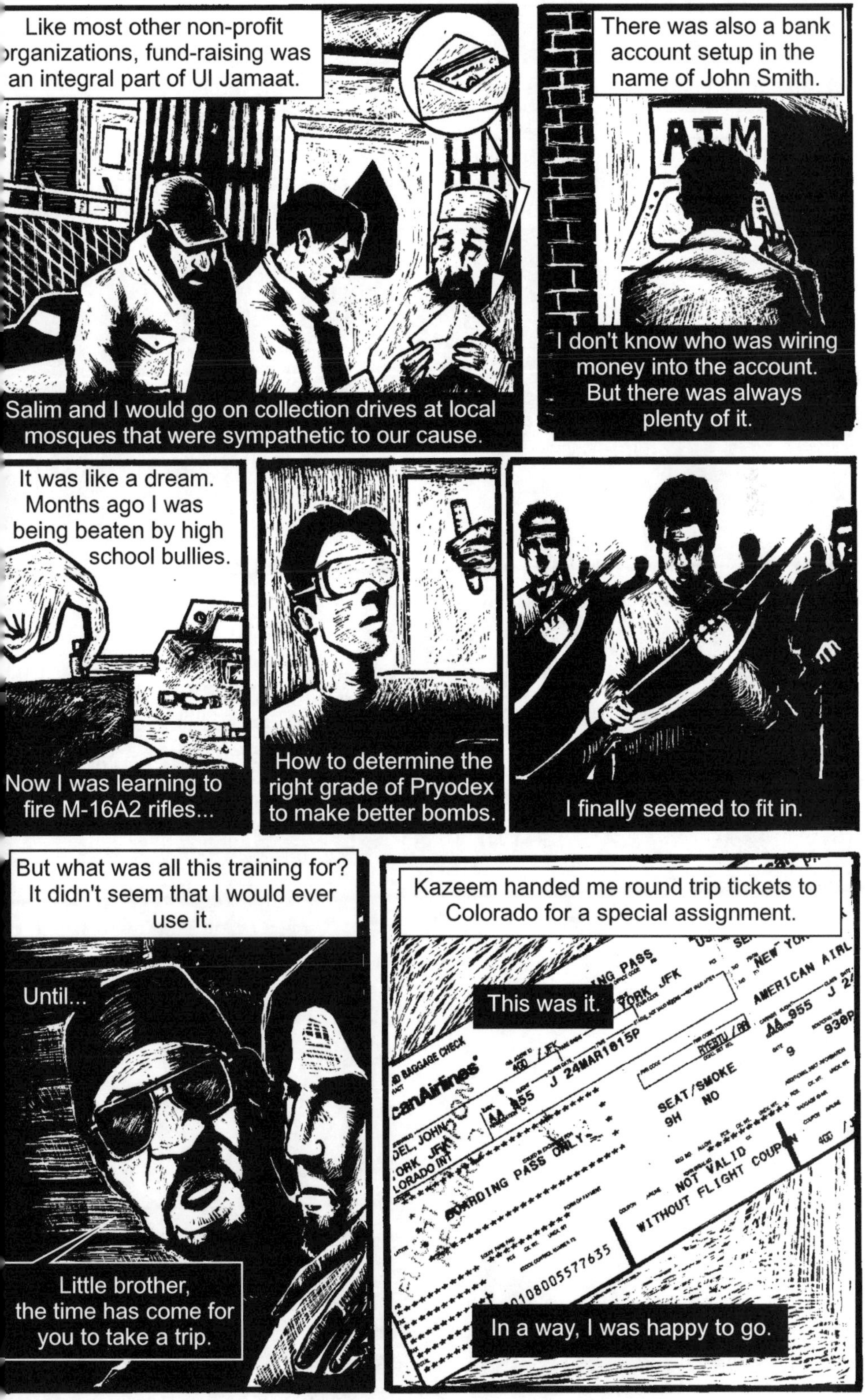

Like most other non-profit organizations, fund-raising was an integral part of Ul Jamaat.
Salim and I would go on collection drives at local mosques that were sympathetic to our cause.
There was also a bank account setup in the name of John Smith.
ATM
I don't know who was wiring money into the account. But there was always plenty of it.
It was like a dream. Months ago I was being beaten by high school bullies.
Now I was learning to fire M-16A2 rifles...
How to determine the right grade of Pryodex to make better bombs.
I finally seemed to fit in.
But what was all this training for? It didn't seem that I would ever use it.
Until...
Little brother, the time has come for you to take a trip.
Kazeem handed me round trip tickets to Colorado for a special assignment.
This was it.
BOARDING PASS ONLY
SEAT/SMOKE
NOT VALID WITHOUT FLIGHT COUPON
In a way, I was happy to go.

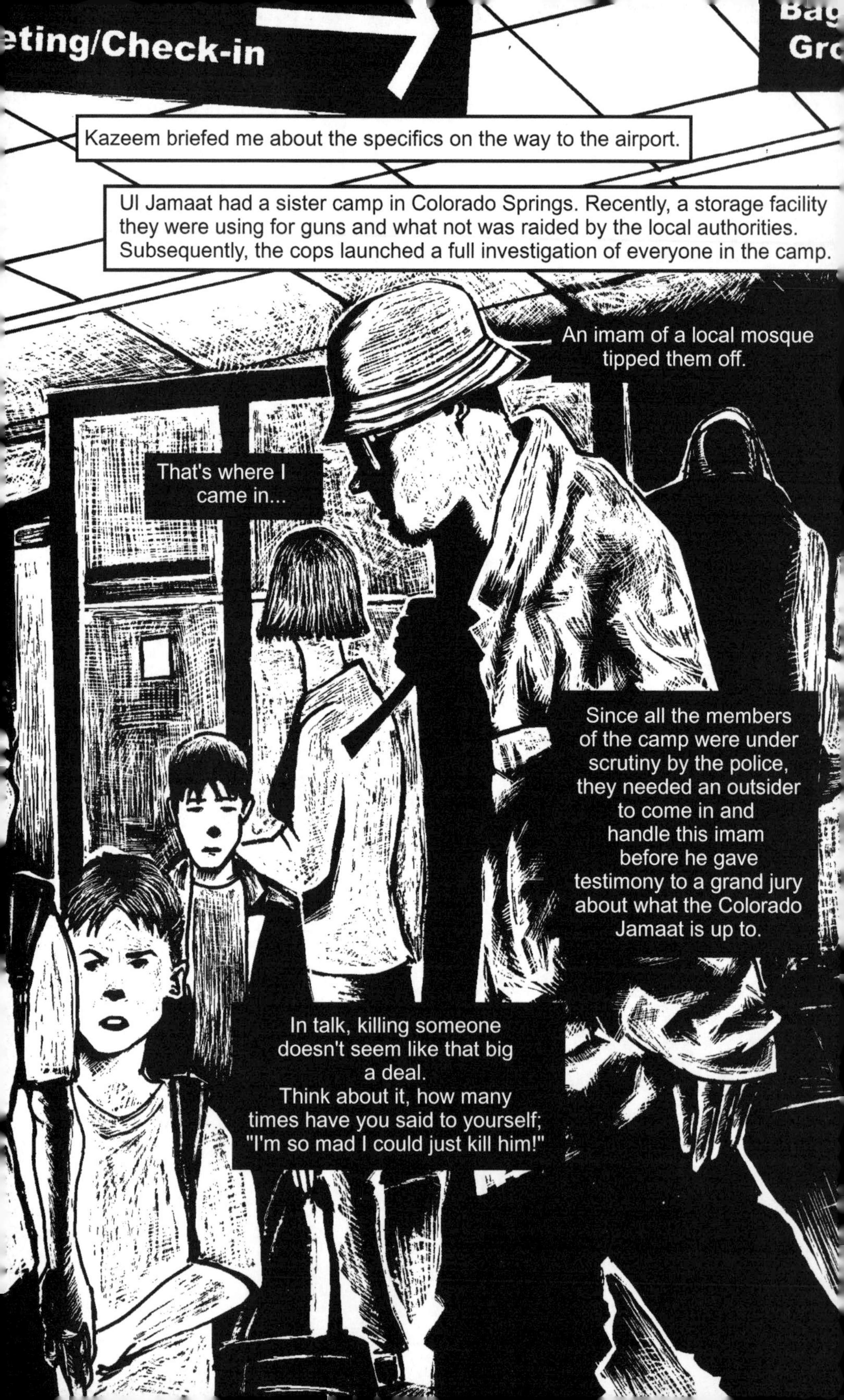

eting/Check-in
Kazeem briefed me about the specifics on the way to the airport.
Ul Jamaat had a sister camp in Colorado Springs. Recently, a storage facility they were using for guns and what not was raided by the local authorities. Subsequently, the cops launched a full investigation of everyone in the camp.
An imam of a local mosque tipped them off.
That's where I came in...
Since all the members of the camp were under scrutiny by the police, they needed an outsider to come in and handle this imam before he gave testimony to a grand jury about what the Colorado Jamaat is up to.
In talk, killing someone doesn't seem like that big a deal.
Think about it, how many times have you said to yourself; "I'm so mad I could just kill him!"

How hard could it be?

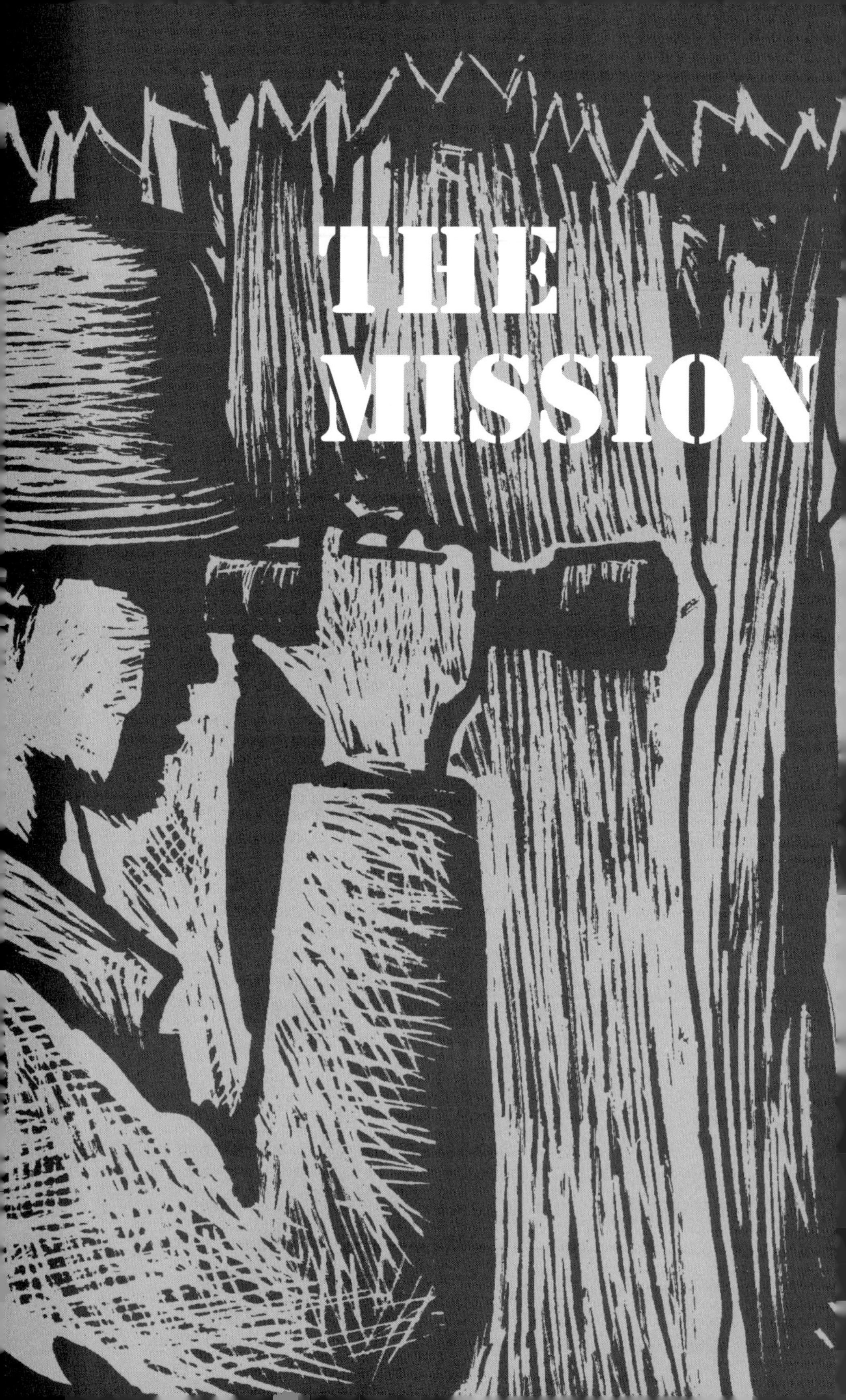
THE
MISSION

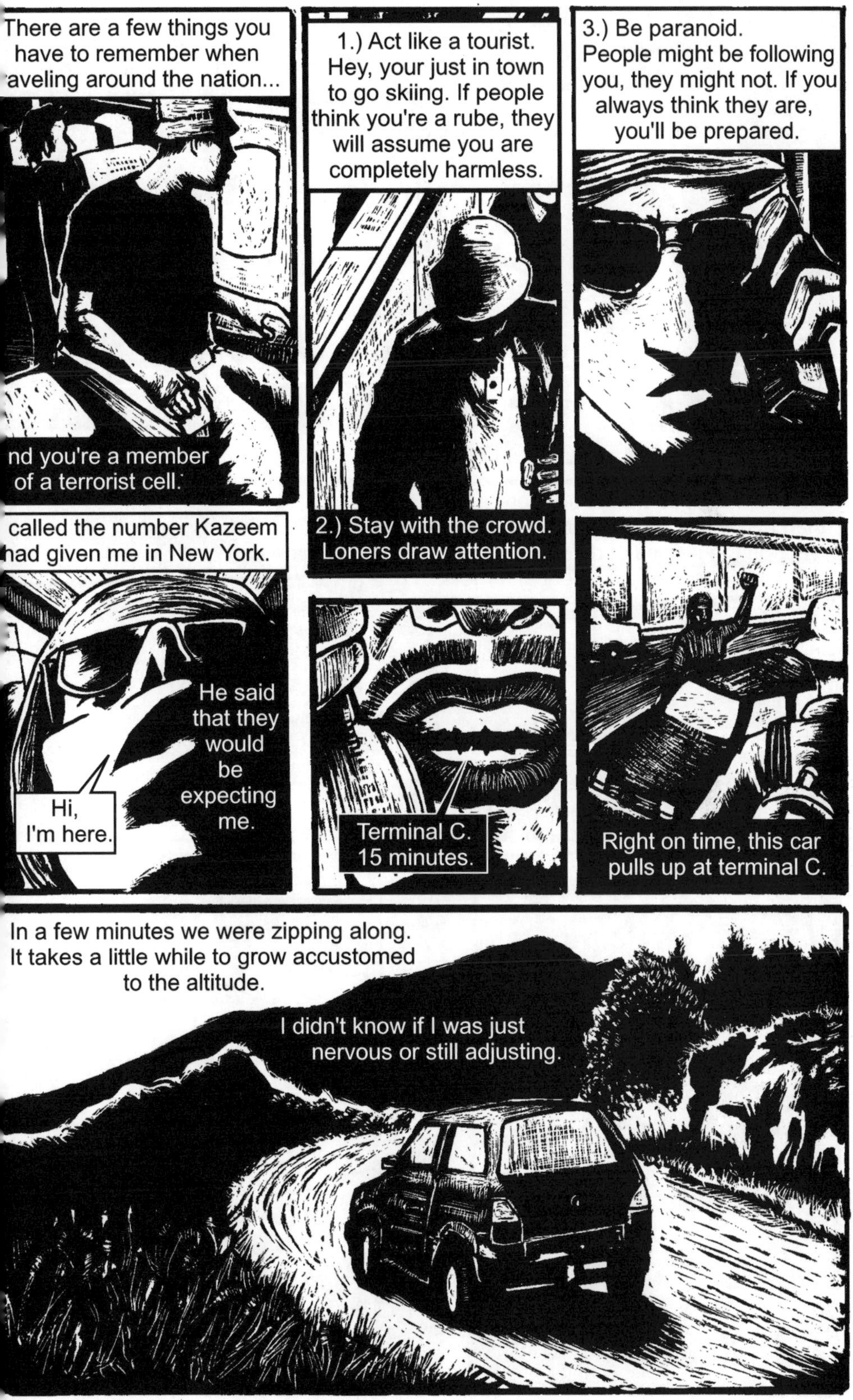

There are a few things you have to remember when 'aveling around the nation...
nd you're a member of a terrorist cell.
1.) Act like a tourist. Hey, your just in town to go skiing. If people think you're a rube, they will assume you are completely harmless.
2.) Stay with the crowd. Loners draw attention.
3.) Be paranoid. People might be following you, they might not. If you always think they are, you'll be prepared.
called the number Kazeem had given me in New York.
Hi, I'm here.
He said that they would be expecting me.
Terminal C. 15 minutes.
Right on time, this car pulls up at terminal C.
In a few minutes we were zipping along. It takes a little while to grow accustomed to the altitude.
I didn't know if I was just nervous or still adjusting.

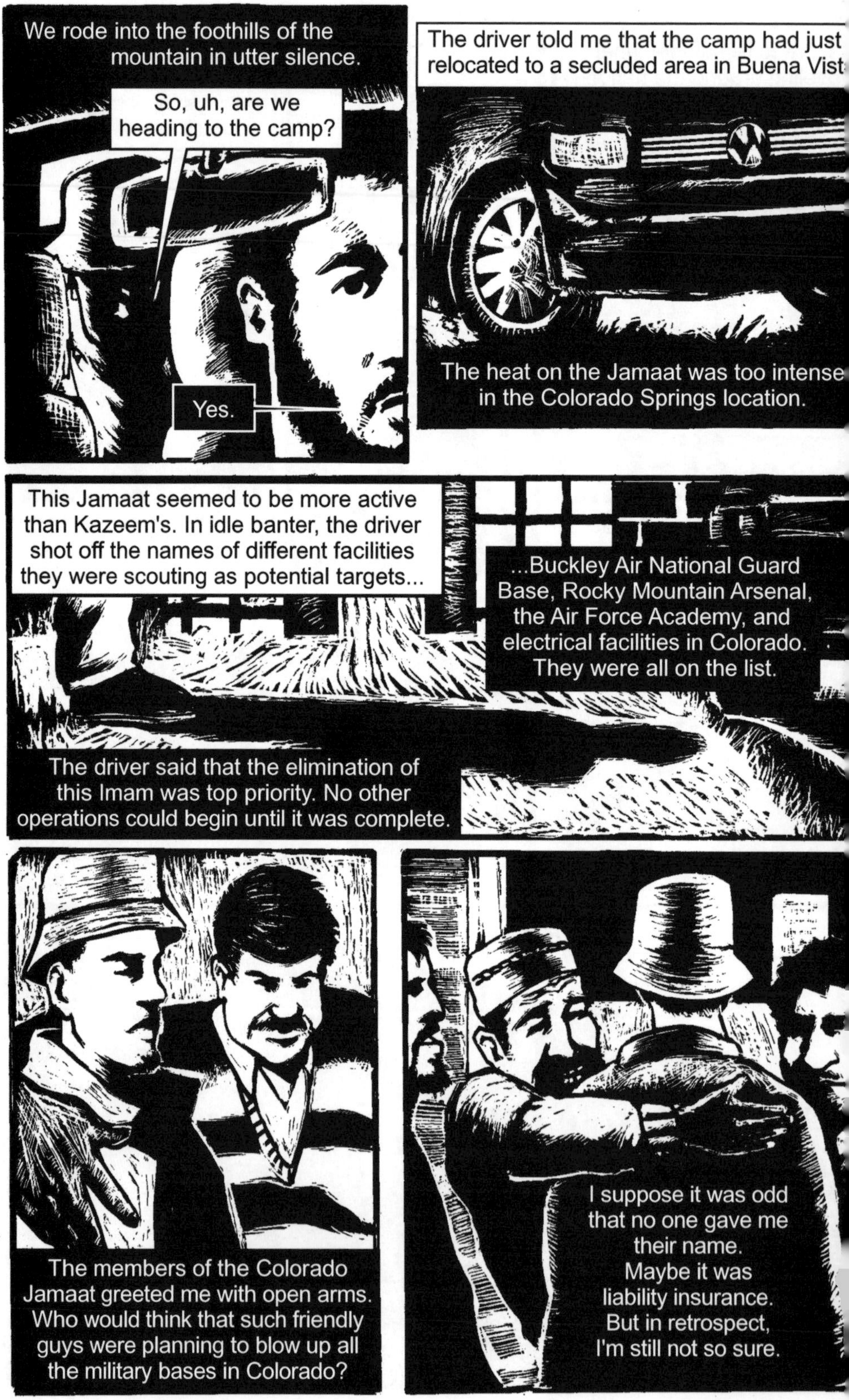
We rode into the foothills of the mountain in utter silence.
So, uh, are we heading to the camp?
Yes.
The driver told me that the camp had just relocated to a secluded area in Buena Vist
The heat on the Jamaat was too intense in the Colorado Springs location.
This Jamaat seemed to be more active than Kazeem's. In idle banter, the driver shot off the names of different facilities they were scouting as potential targets...
...Buckley Air National Guard Base, Rocky Mountain Arsenal, the Air Force Academy, and electrical facilities in Colorado. They were all on the list.
The driver said that the elimination of this Imam was top priority. No other operations could begin until it was complete.
The members of the Colorado Jamaat greeted me with open arms. Who would think that such friendly guys were planning to blow up all the military bases in Colorado?
I suppose it was odd that no one gave me their name. Maybe it was liability insurance. But in retrospect, I'm still not so sure.

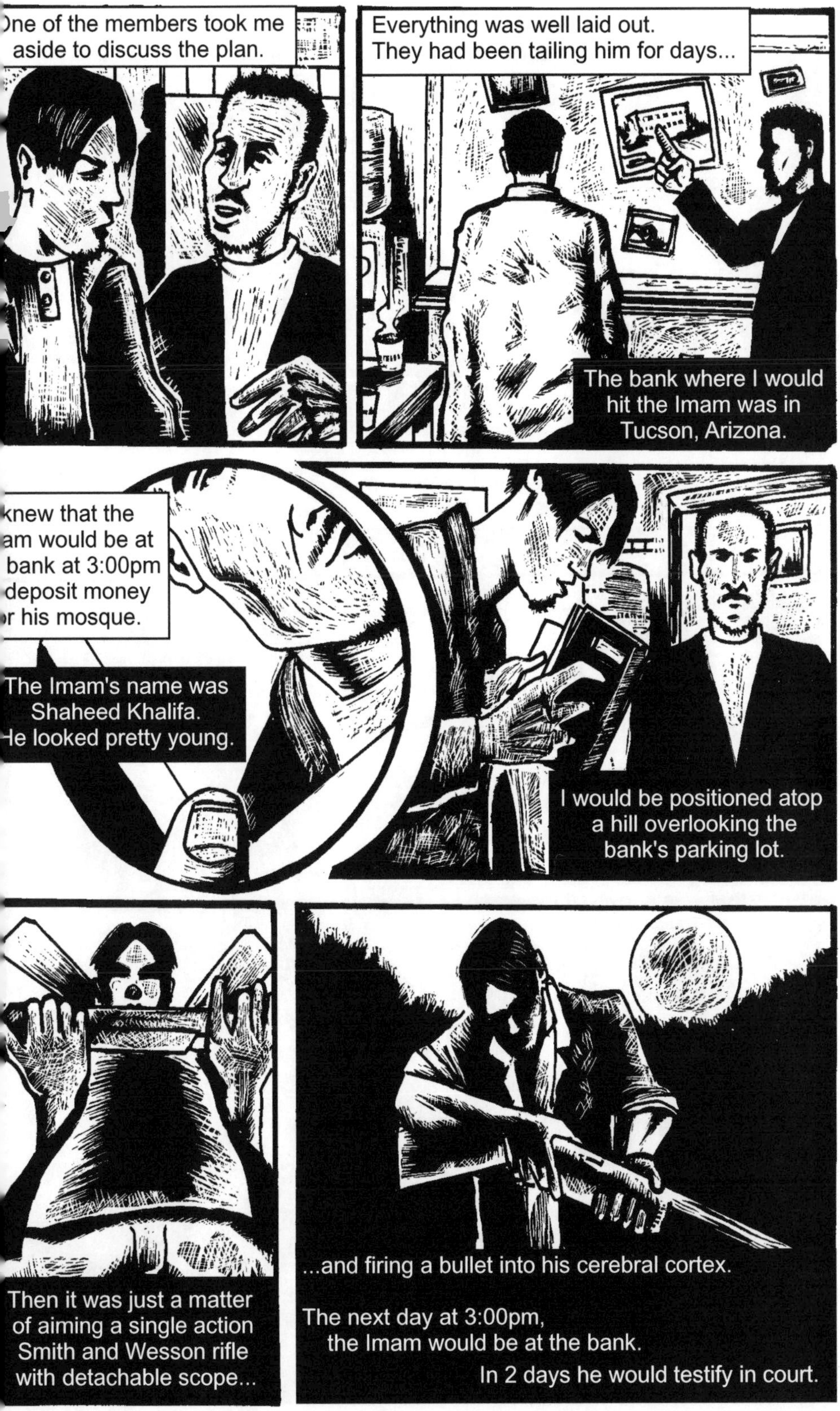
ne of the members took me aside to discuss the plan.
Everything was well laid out. They had been tailing him for days...
The bank where I would hit the Imam was in Tucson, Arizona.
knew that the am would be at bank at 3:00pm deposit money r his mosque.
The Imam's name was Shaheed Khalifa. le looked pretty young.
I would be positioned atop a hill overlooking the bank's parking lot.
Then it was just a matter of aiming a single action Smith and Wesson rifle with detachable scope...
...and firing a bullet into his cerebral cortex.
The next day at 3:00pm, the Imam would be at the bank.
In 2 days he would testify in court.

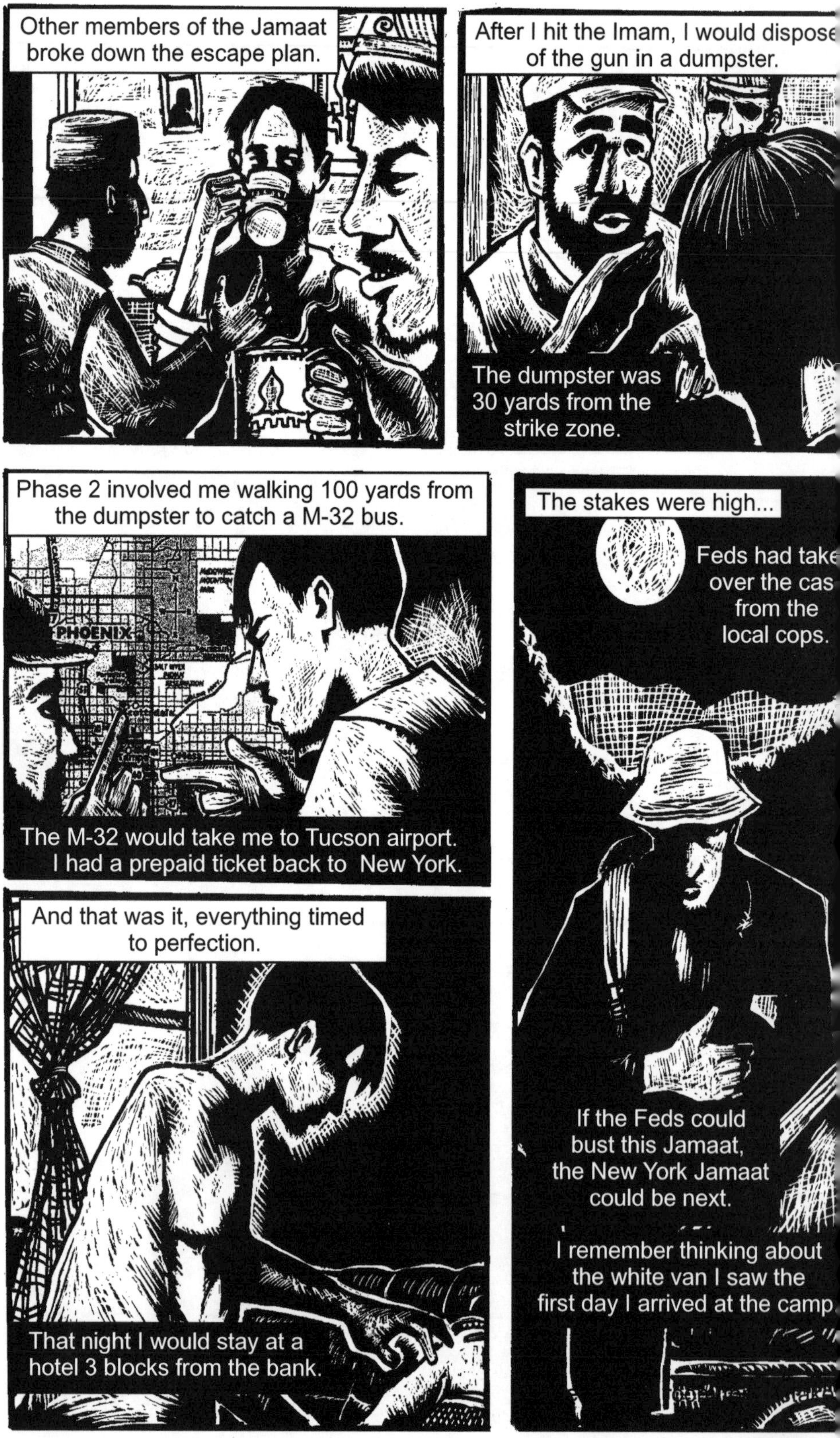
Other members of the Jamaat broke down the escape plan.
After I hit the Imam, I would dispose of the gun in a dumpster.
The dumpster was 30 yards from the strike zone.
Phase 2 involved me walking 100 yards from the dumpster to catch a M-32 bus.
PHOENIX
The M-32 would take me to Tucson airport. I had a prepaid ticket back to New York.
And that was it, everything timed to perfection.
That night I would stay at a hotel 3 blocks from the bank.
The stakes were high...
Feds had take over the cas from the local cops.
If the Feds could bust this Jamaat, the New York Jamaat could be next.
I remember thinking about the white van I saw the first day I arrived at the camp.

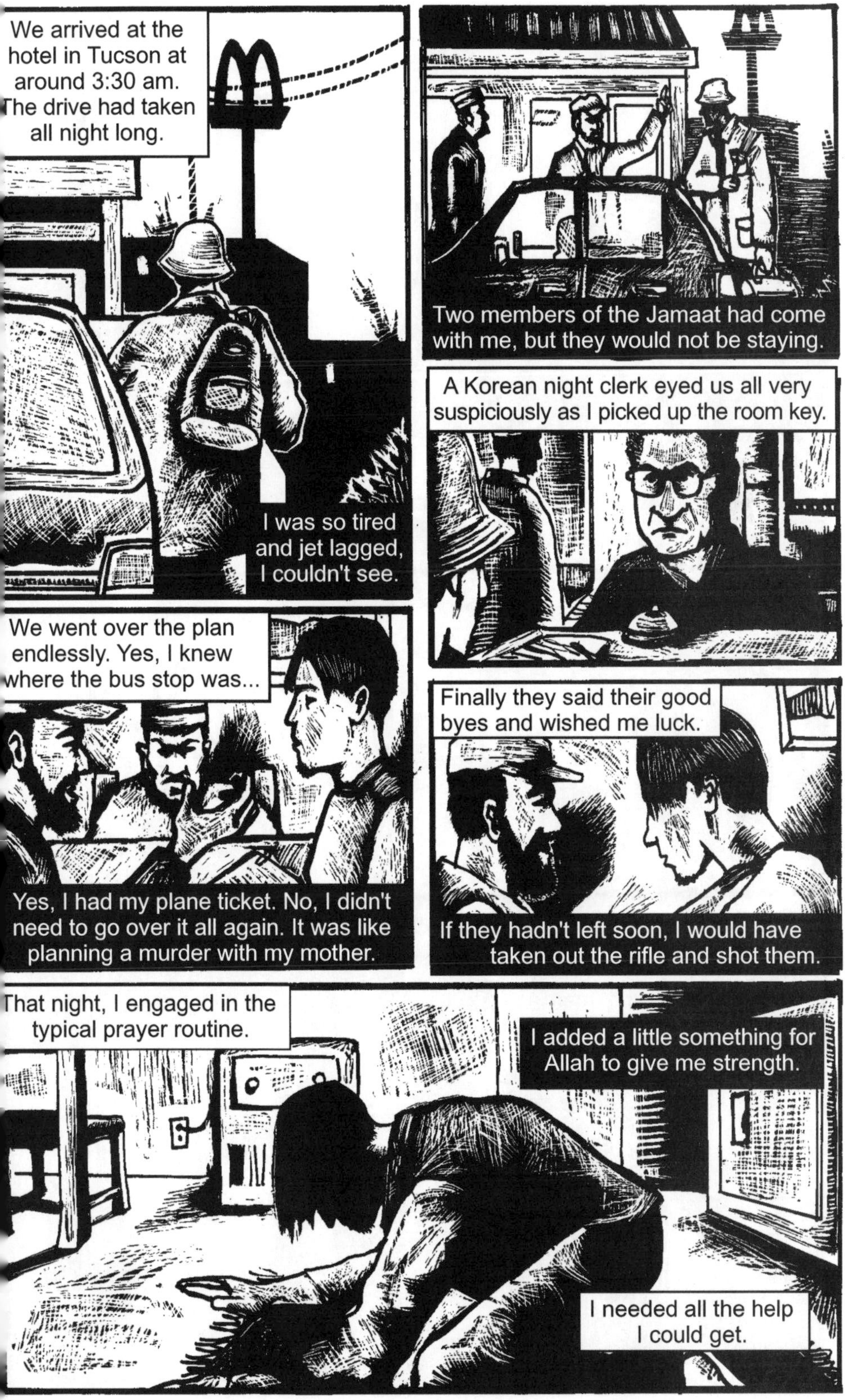
We arrived at the hotel in Tucson at around 3:30 am. The drive had taken all night long.
I was so tired and jet lagged, I couldn't see.
Two members of the Jamaat had come with me, but they would not be staying.
A Korean night clerk eyed us all very suspiciously as I picked up the room key.
We went over the plan endlessly. Yes, I knew where the bus stop was...
Yes, I had my plane ticket. No, I didn't need to go over it all again. It was like planning a murder with my mother.
Finally they said their good byes and wished me luck.
If they hadn't left soon, I would have taken out the rifle and shot them.
That night, I engaged in the typical prayer routine.
I added a little something for Allah to give me strength.
I needed all the help I could get.

The next day I awoke at 12:00 pm. I hadn't really slept at all. All I needed was some khat to give me the jolt I needed for that afternoon.

The clerk I had gotten the room key from the night before was still on duty.

The weird fucker kept giving me looks as I left.

I decided to walk past the M-32 stop.

BUS

The plan was ingrained in my head.

I could sleepwa throug it.

The location was perfect. Just enough foliage to keep me out of view from the parking lot.

I methodically began to assemble the rifle I had brought in a gym bag

A feeling of reassuranc surged through me wit every snap and click.

The only thing left to do was sit and wait for the Imam's candy-apple red Toyota Corolla to enter the lot.

I detached the scope from the rifle to survey the parking lot.

1:23 pm.

I still had a good hour and a half before the Imam would arrive.

After an hour and 15 minutes of sitting and twitching from the khat, I spot a red Corolla.

Candy apple red, Colorado license plates.

The roads are plagued with these god-awful Corollas.

I had to be sure...

A man got out that looked like the Imam.

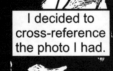

I decided to cross-reference the photo I had.

Hello Shaheed Khalifa.

It was definitely the right guy.
He was only 15 minutes early.
This was it.
The moment of truth.
I had been training nearly a year for this.

I thought back to hunting in the woods with my father...

My nerves were steel. I've read that soldiers often felt a wave of calmness in the grip of battle.
I felt calm.
There was only one thing left to do...

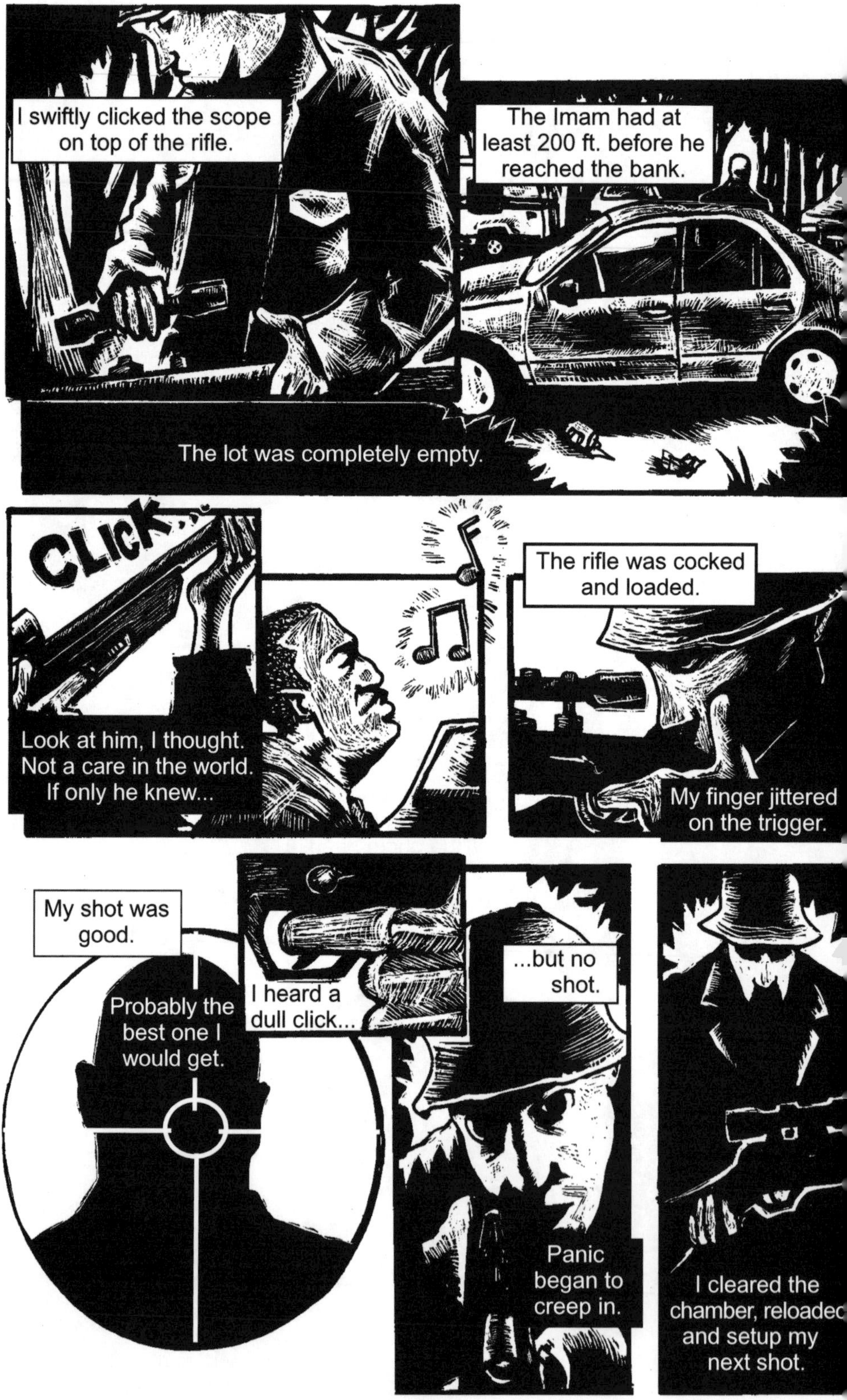
I swiftly clicked the scope on top of the rifle.
The Imam had at least 200 ft. before he reached the bank.
The lot was completely empty.
CLICK
Look at him, I thought. Not a care in the world. If only he knew...
The rifle was cocked and loaded.
My finger jittered on the trigger.
My shot was good.
Probably the best one I would get.
I heard a dull click...
...but no shot.
Panic began to creep in.
I cleared the chamber, reloadec and setup my next shot.

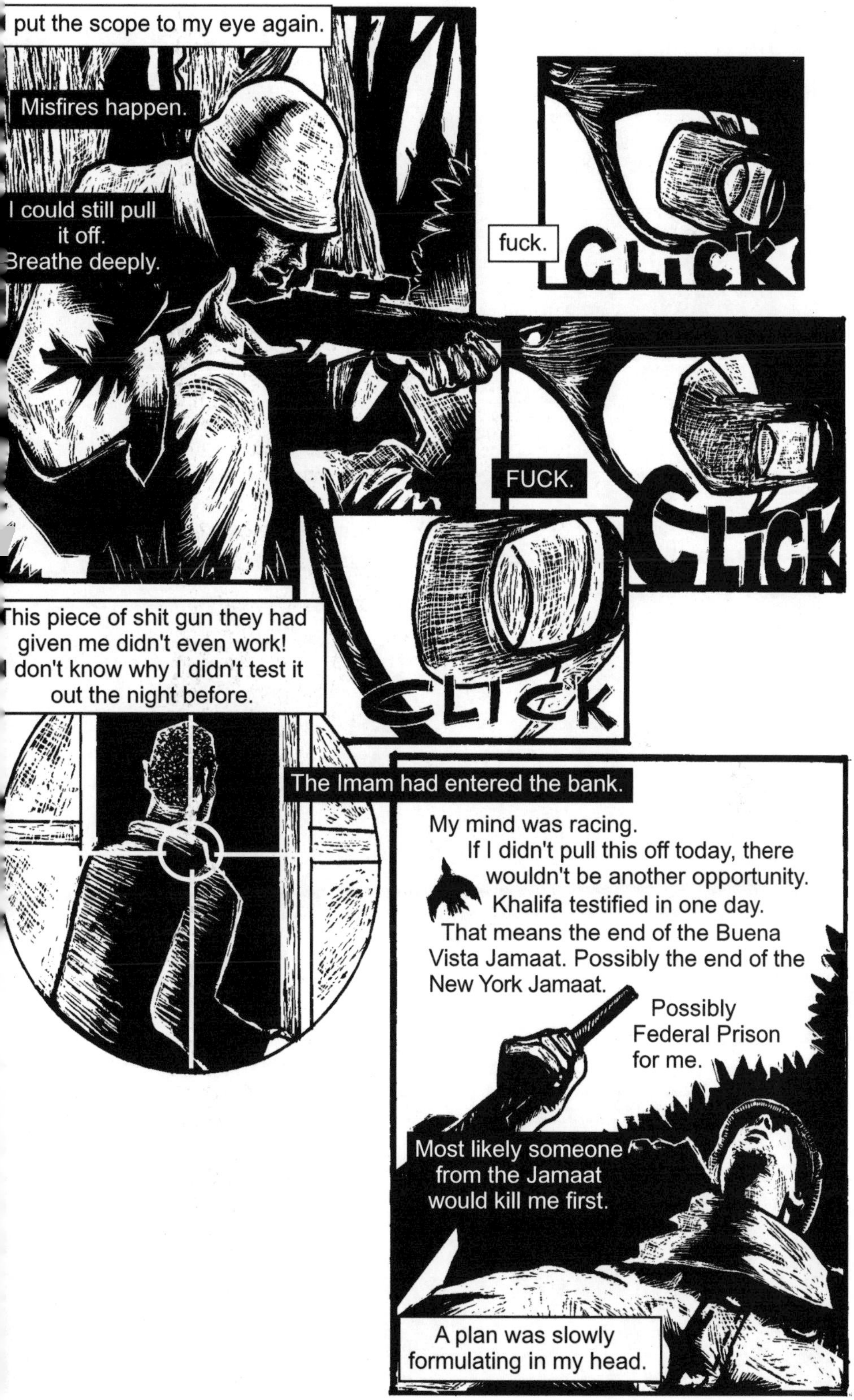

I put the scope to my eye again.
Misfires happen.
I could still pull it off.
Breathe deeply.
fuck.
CLICK
FUCK.
CLICK
CLICK
This piece of shit gun they had given me didn't even work!
I don't know why I didn't test it out the night before.
The Imam had entered the bank.
My mind was racing.
If I didn't pull this off today, there wouldn't be another opportunity.
Khalifa testified in one day.
That means the end of the Buena Vista Jamaat. Possibly the end of the New York Jamaat.
Possibly Federal Prison for me.
Most likely someone from the Jamaat would kill me first.
A plan was slowly formulating in my head.

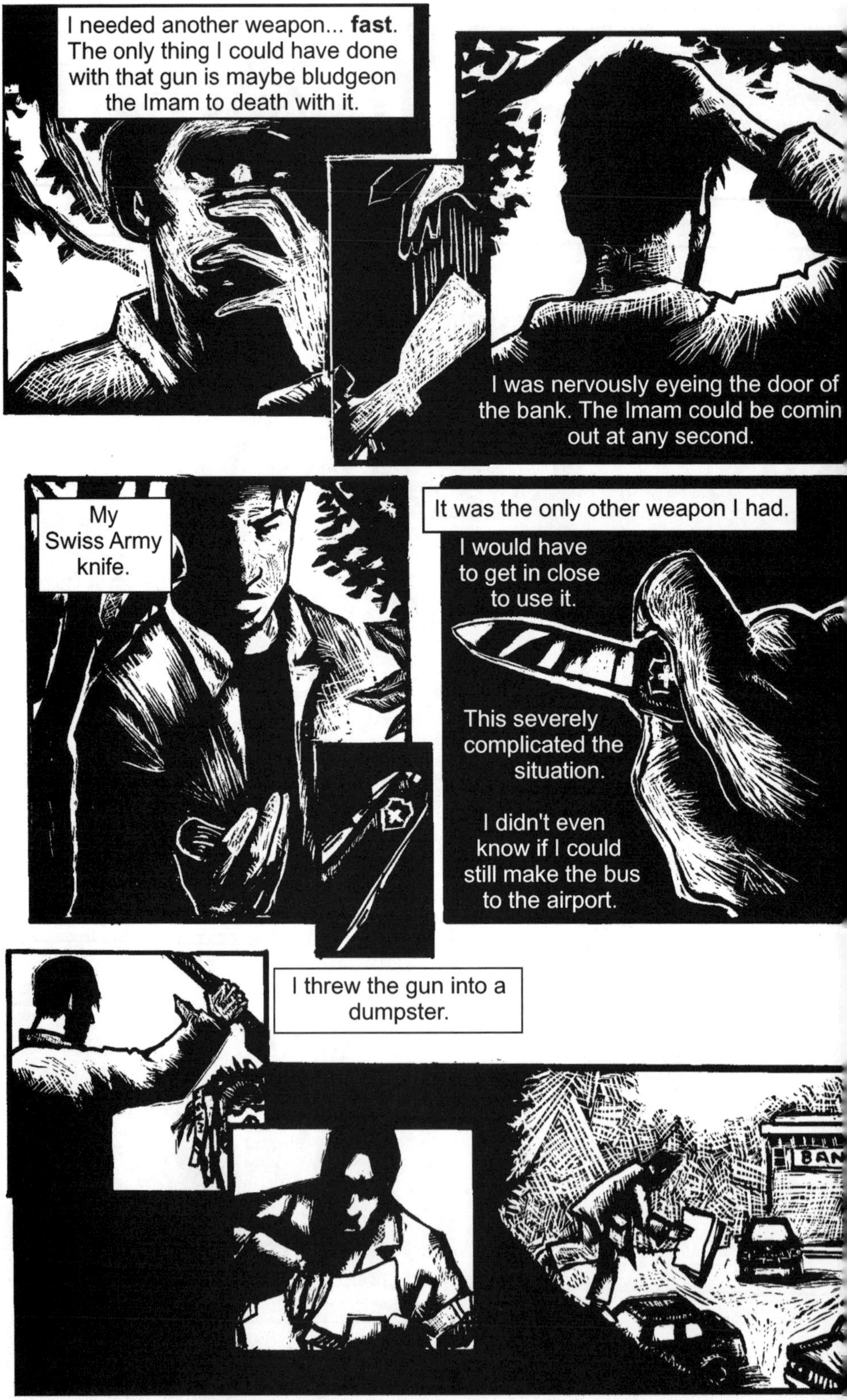

I needed another weapon... **fast**. The only thing I could have done with that gun is maybe bludgeon the Imam to death with it.
I was nervously eyeing the door of the bank. The Imam could be comin out at any second.
My Swiss Army knife.
It was the only other weapon I had.
I would have to get in close to use it.
This severely complicated the situation.
I didn't even know if I could still make the bus to the airport.
I threw the gun into a dumpster.

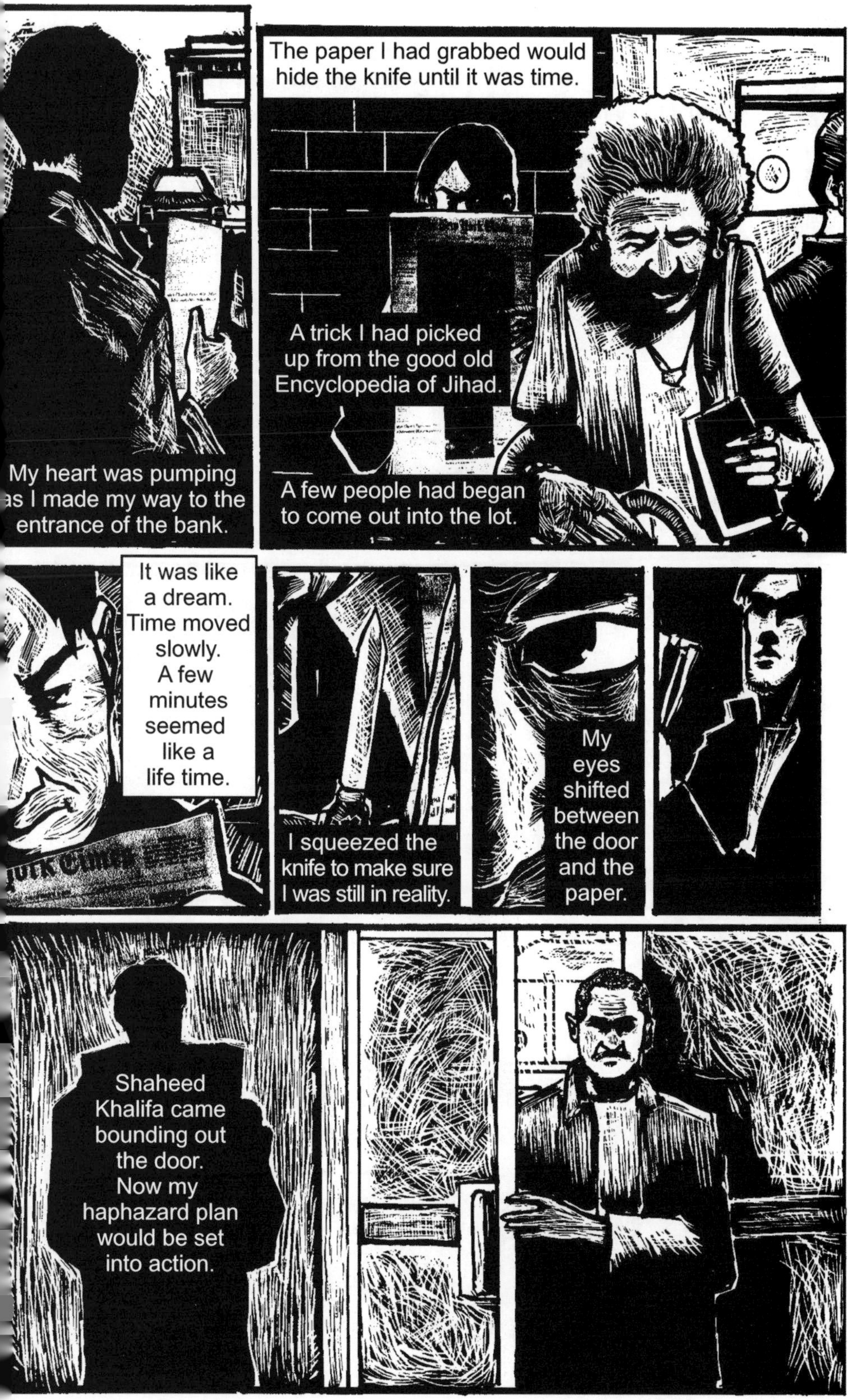
My heart was pumping as I made my way to the entrance of the bank.
The paper I had grabbed would hide the knife until it was time.
A trick I had picked up from the good old Encyclopedia of Jihad.
A few people had began to come out into the lot.
It was like a dream. Time moved slowly. A few minutes seemed like a life time.
I squeezed the knife to make sure I was still in reality.
My eyes shifted between the door and the paper.
Shaheed Khalifa came bounding out the door. Now my haphazard plan would be set into action.

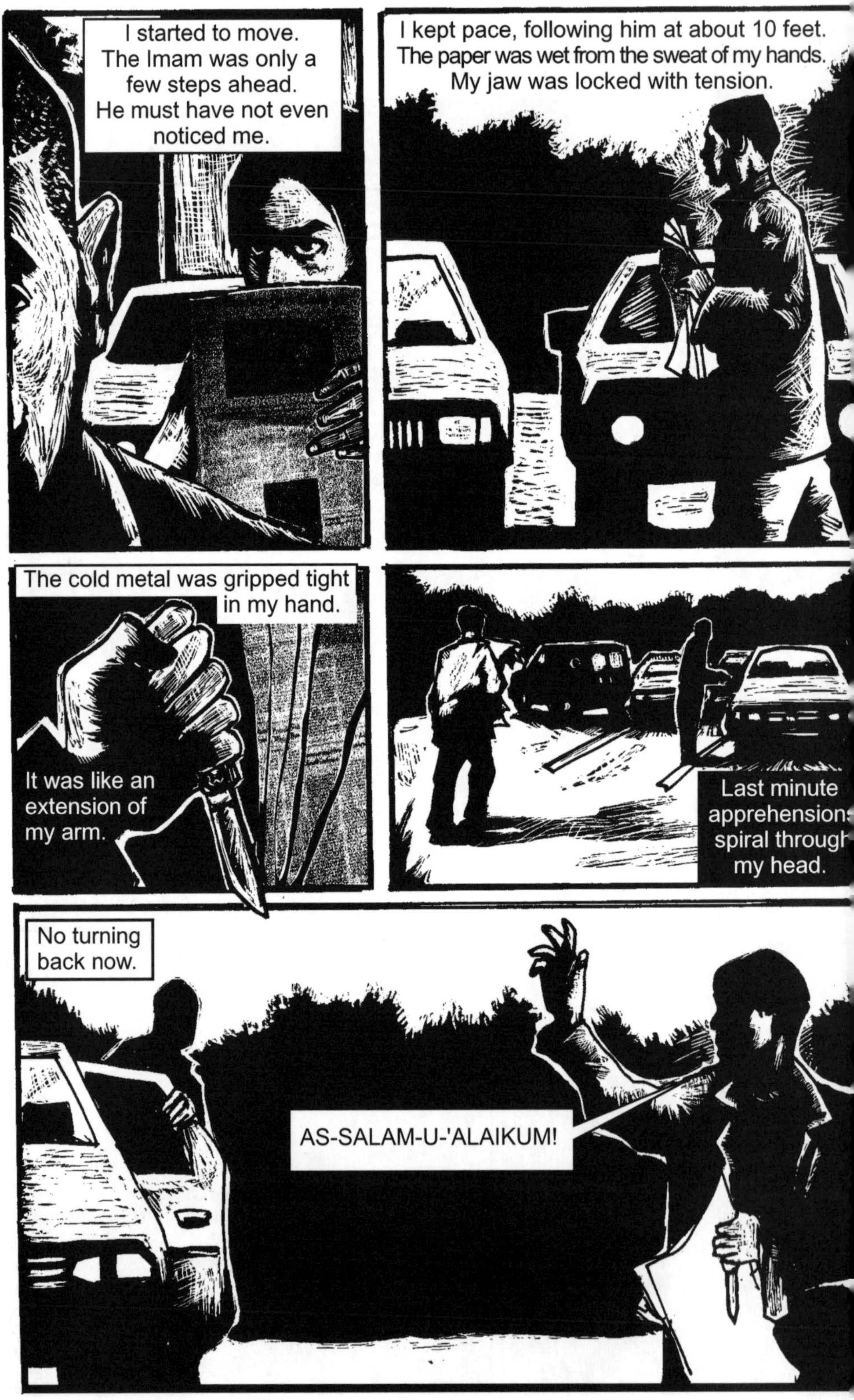
I started to move. The Imam was only a few steps ahead. He must have not even noticed me.
I kept pace, following him at about 10 feet. The paper was wet from the sweat of my hands. My jaw was locked with tension.
The cold metal was gripped tight in my hand.
It was like an extension of my arm.
Last minute apprehension spiral through my head.
No turning back now.
AS-SALAM-U-'ALAIKUM!

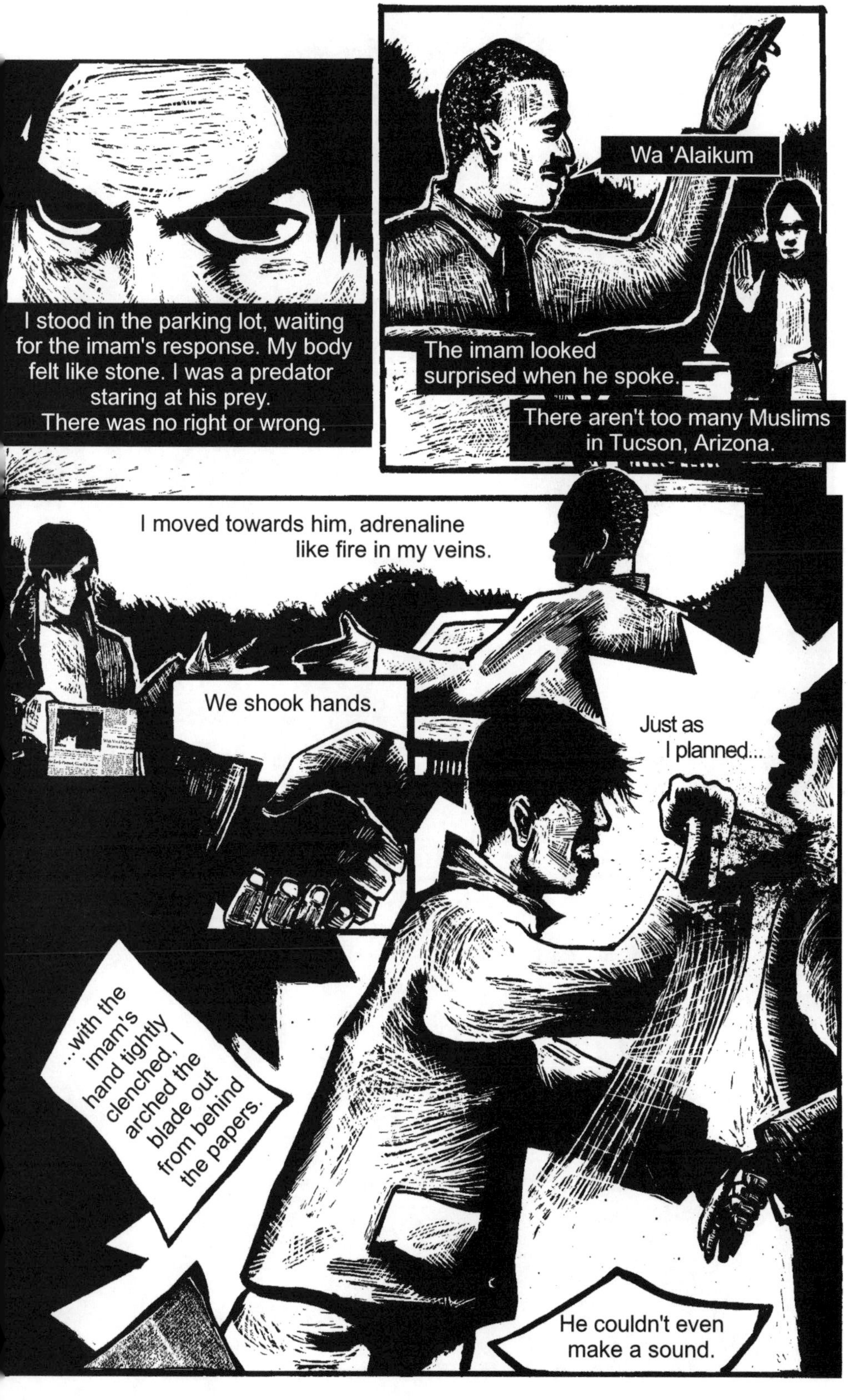
I stood in the parking lot, waiting for the imam's response. My body felt like stone. I was a predator staring at his prey. There was no right or wrong.
Wa 'Alaikum
The imam looked surprised when he spoke.
There aren't too many Muslims in Tucson, Arizona.
I moved towards him, adrenaline like fire in my veins.
We shook hands.
Just as I planned...
...with the imam's hand tightly clenched, I arched the blade out from behind the papers.
He couldn't even make a sound.

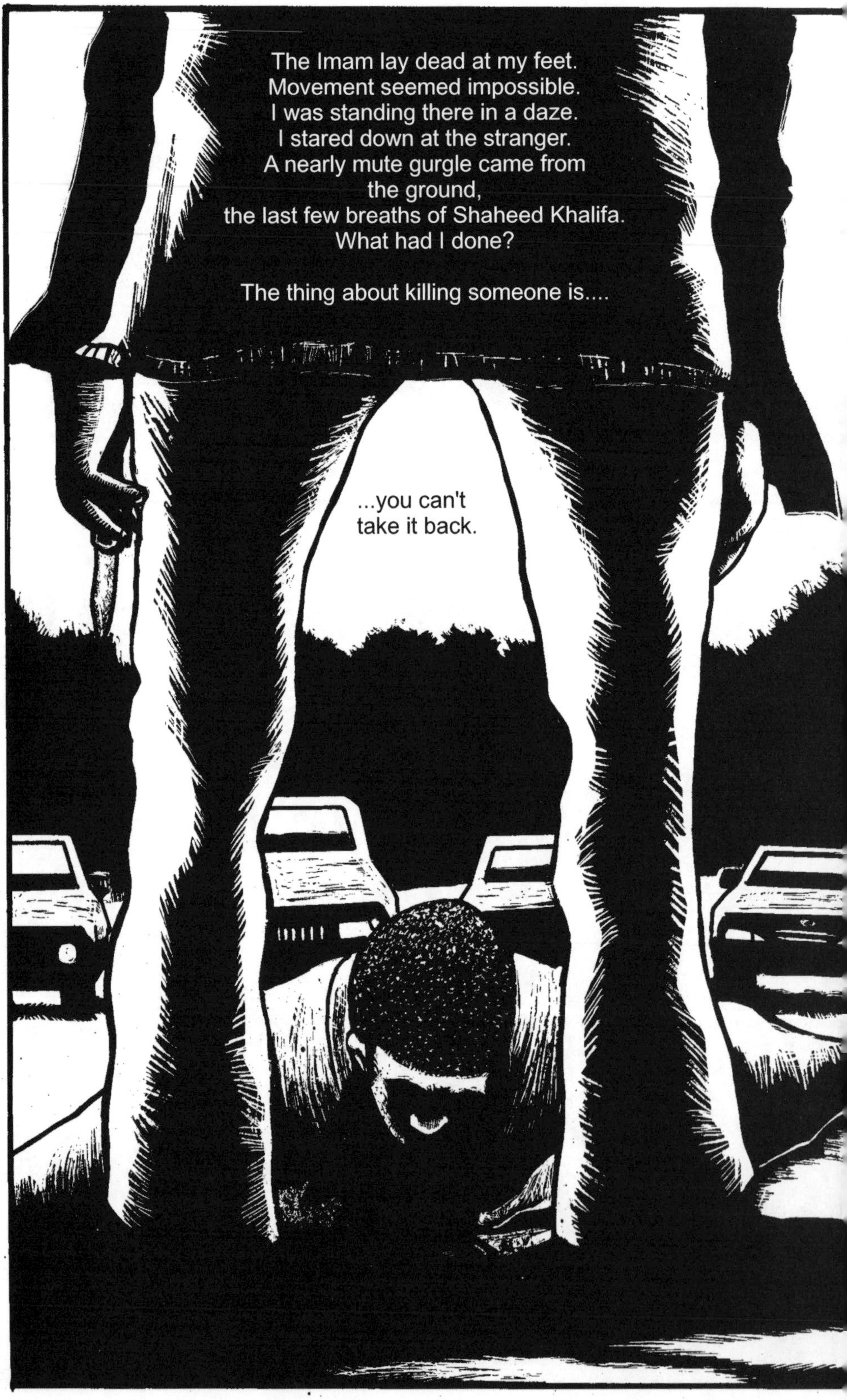
The Imam lay dead at my feet.
Movement seemed impossible.
I was standing there in a daze.
I stared down at the stranger.
A nearly mute gurgle came from the ground,
the last few breaths of Shaheed Khalifa.
What had I done?
The thing about killing someone is....
...you can't take it back.

I cautiously lifted Khalifa's body into the open driver's side door.

It appeared that my actions had gone undetected.

Blood cascaded down his shirt from the massive neck wound.

must have been covered with it.

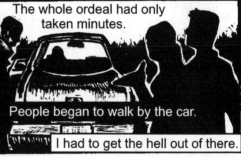

The whole ordeal had only taken minutes.

People began to walk by the car.

I had to get the hell out of there.

All remorse and nostalgia had to be put on pause.

The survival instinct kicked in.

First there was the matter of my blood soaked clothes.

There was no way they were going to let me on a plane looking like Jack the Ripper.

There were people milling about all around me.

I had to clean up.

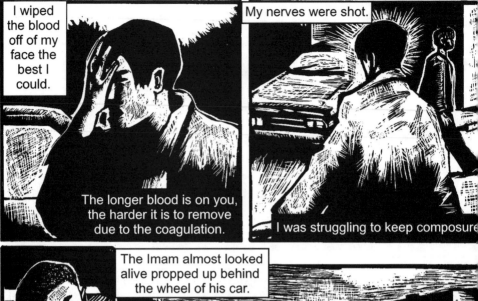

I wiped the blood off of my face the best I could.

The longer blood is on you, the harder it is to remove due to the coagulation.

My nerves were shot.

I was struggling to keep composure.

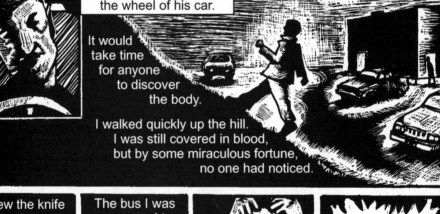

The Imam almost looked alive propped up behind the wheel of his car.

It would take time for anyone to discover the body.

I walked quickly up the hill. I was still covered in blood, but by some miraculous fortune, no one had noticed.

I threw the knife into the dumpster.

This dumpster was becoming a treasure-trove of evidence against me.

The bus I was supposed to make had come and gone.

I removed my shirt.

It was stiff with blood.

I threw it into the woods.

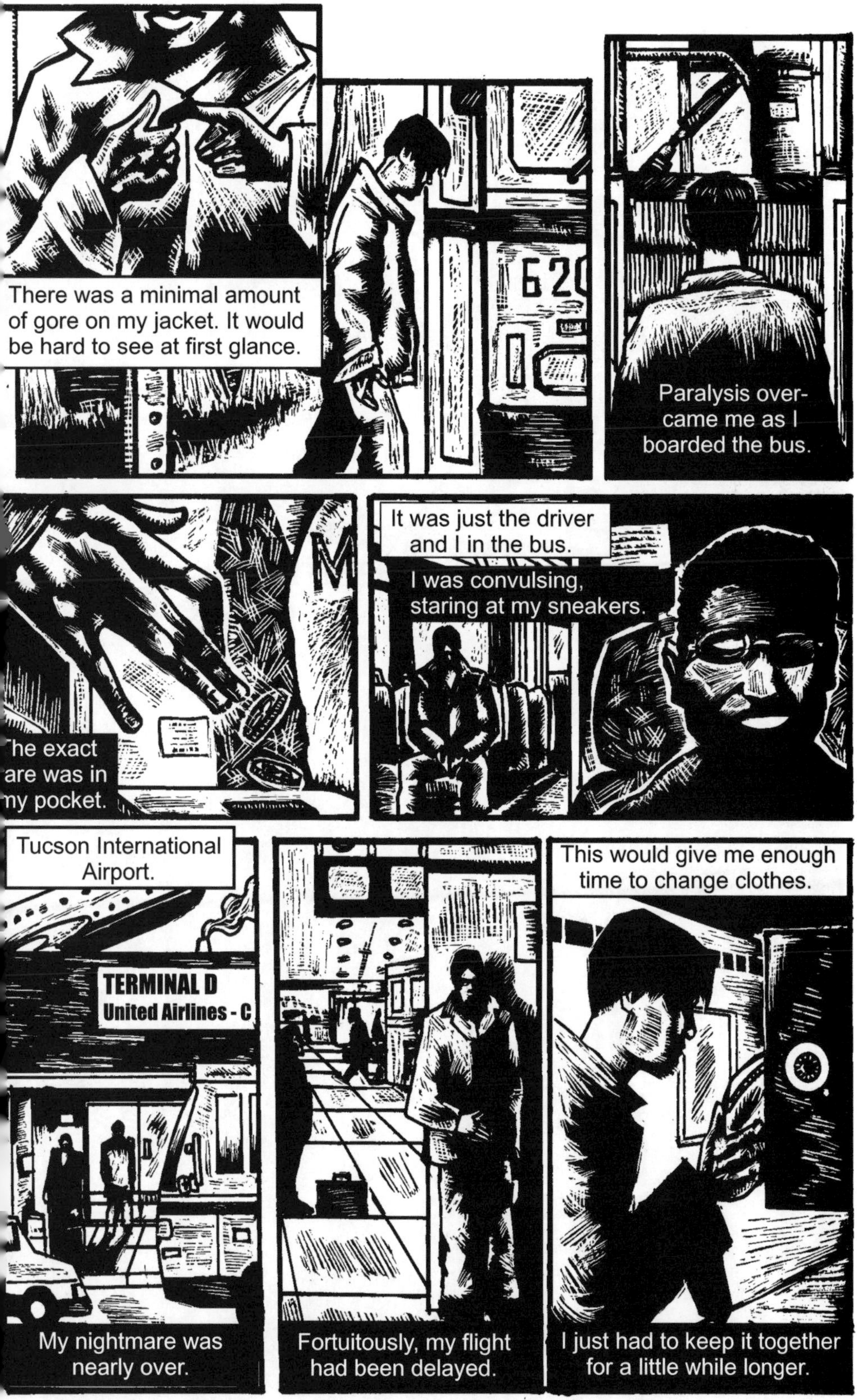

There was a minimal amount of gore on my jacket. It would be hard to see at first glance.
62
Paralysis over-came me as I boarded the bus.
M
he exact are was in my pocket.
It was just the driver and I in the bus.
I was convulsing, staring at my sneakers.
Tucson International Airport.
TERMINAL D
United Airlines - C
My nightmare was nearly over.
Fortuitously, my flight had been delayed.
This would give me enough time to change clothes.
I just had to keep it together for a little while longer.

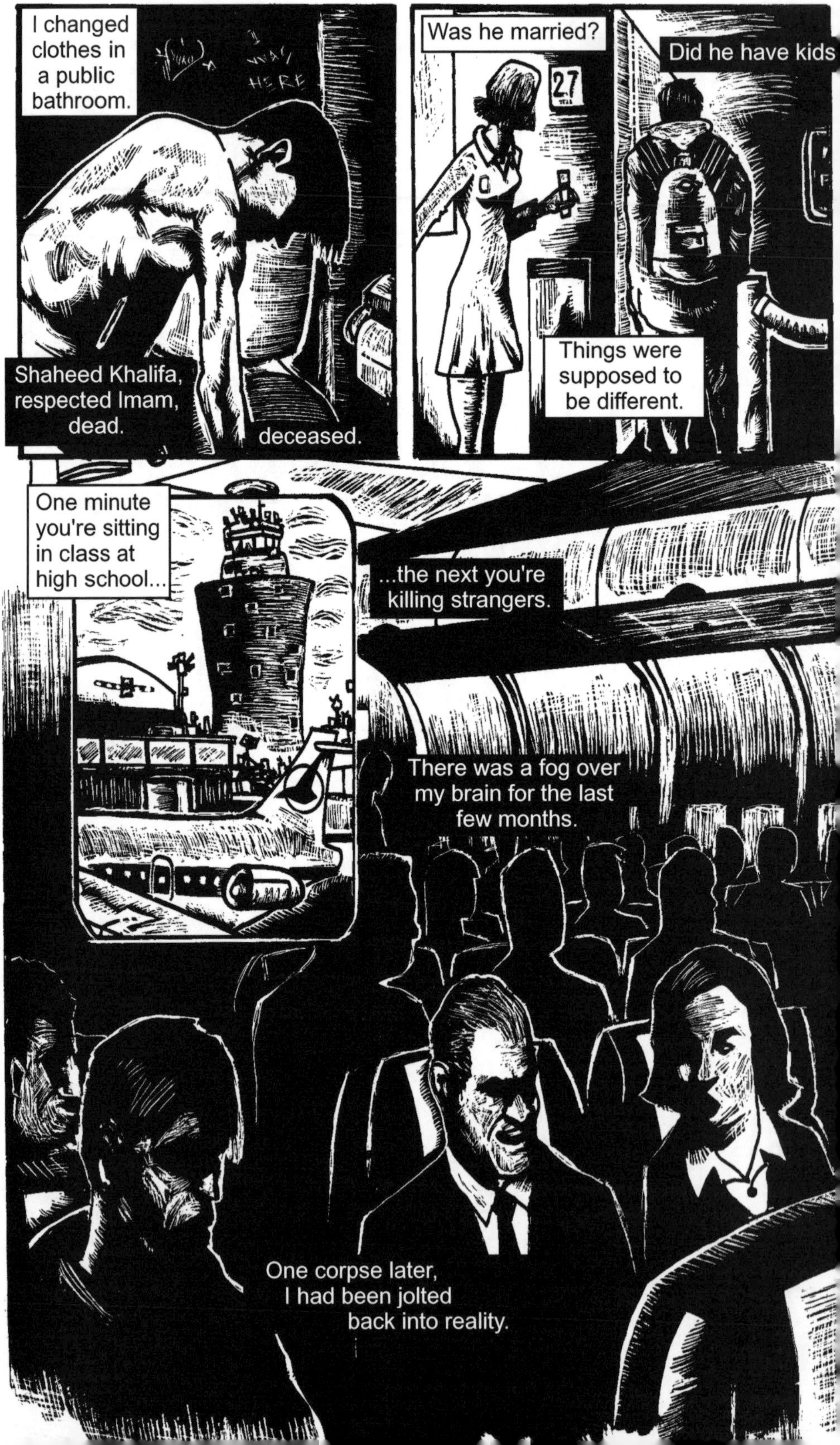
I changed clothes in a public bathroom.
I WAS HERE
Shaheed Khalifa, respected Imam, dead.
deceased.
Was he married?
27
Did he have kids
Things were supposed to be different.
One minute you're sitting in class at high school...
...the next you're killing strangers.
There was a fog over my brain for the last few months.
One corpse later, I had been jolted back into reality.

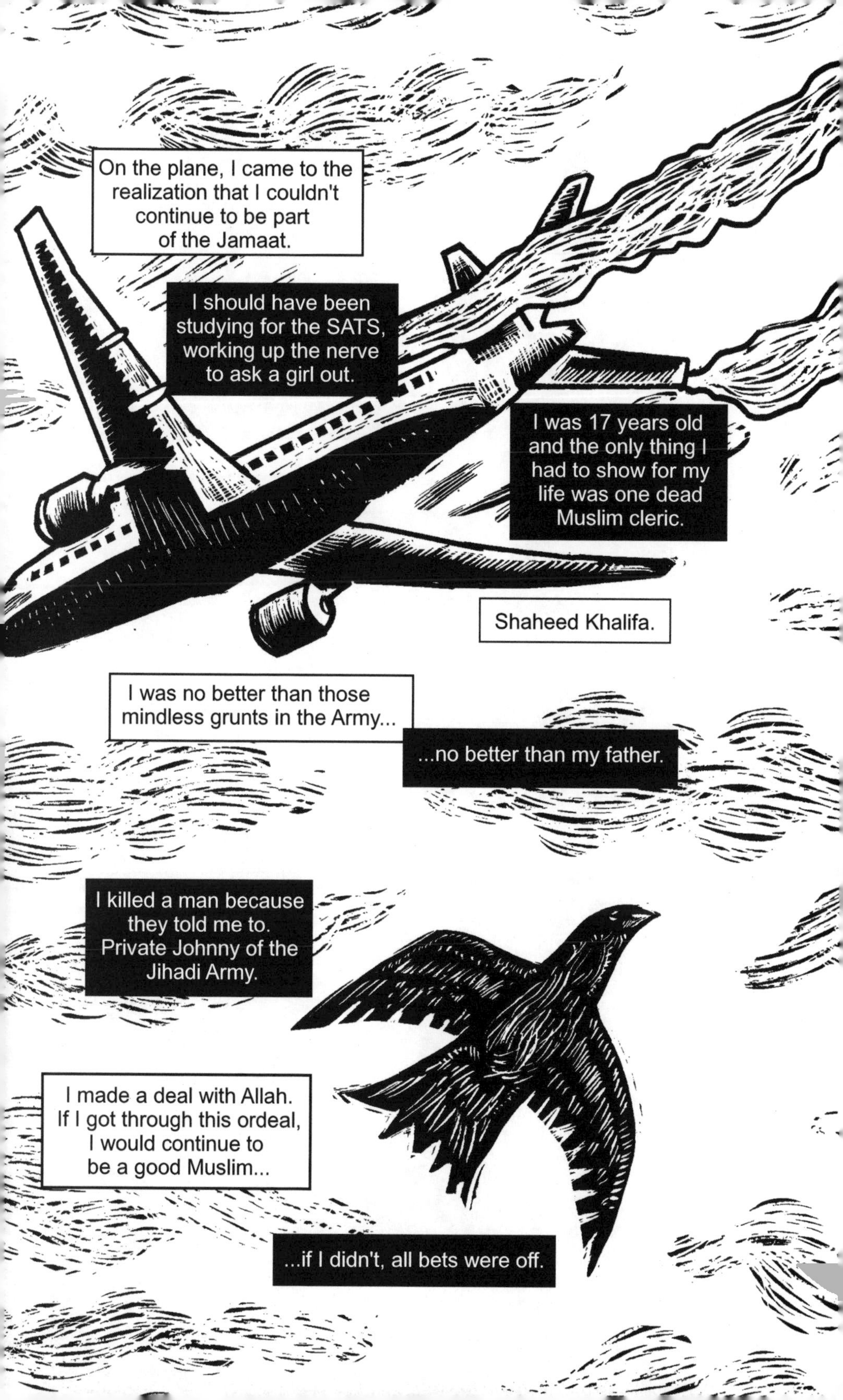
On the plane, I came to the realization that I couldn't continue to be part of the Jamaat.
I should have been studying for the SATS, working up the nerve to ask a girl out.
I was 17 years old and the only thing I had to show for my life was one dead Muslim cleric.
Shaheed Khalifa.
I was no better than those mindless grunts in the Army...
...no better than my father.
I killed a man because they told me to. Private Johnny of the Jihadi Army.
I made a deal with Allah. If I got through this ordeal, I would continue to be a good Muslim...
...if I didn't, all bets were off.

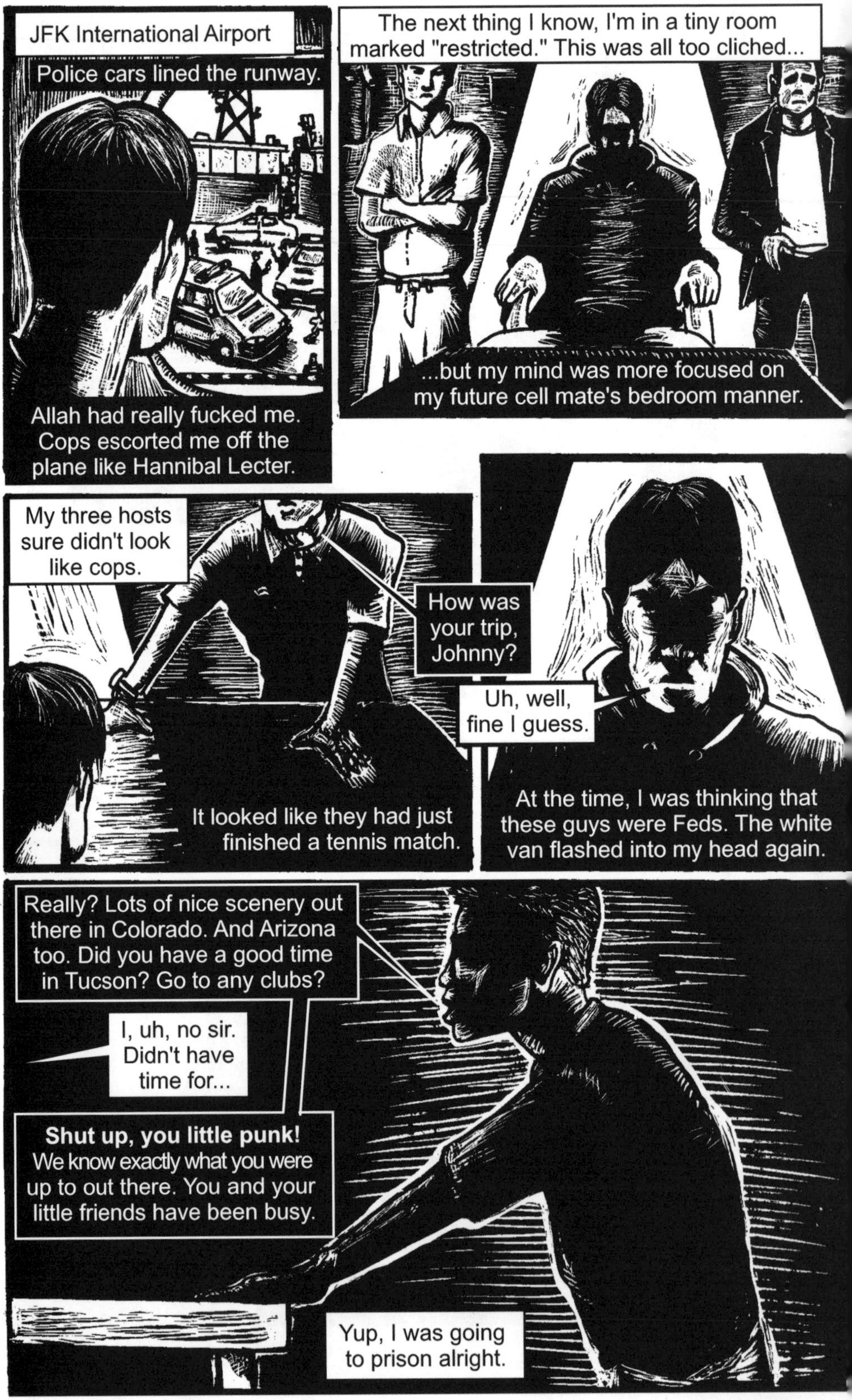

JFK International Airport
Police cars lined the runway.
Allah had really fucked me. Cops escorted me off the plane like Hannibal Lecter.
The next thing I know, I'm in a tiny room marked "restricted." This was all too cliched...
...but my mind was more focused on my future cell mate's bedroom manner.
My three hosts sure didn't look like cops.
How was your trip, Johnny?
It looked like they had just finished a tennis match.
Uh, well, fine I guess.
At the time, I was thinking that these guys were Feds. The white van flashed into my head again.
Really? Lots of nice scenery out there in Colorado. And Arizona too. Did you have a good time in Tucson? Go to any clubs?
I, uh, no sir. Didn't have time for...
Shut up, you little punk! We know exactly what you were up to out there. You and your little friends have been busy.
Yup, I was going to prison alright.

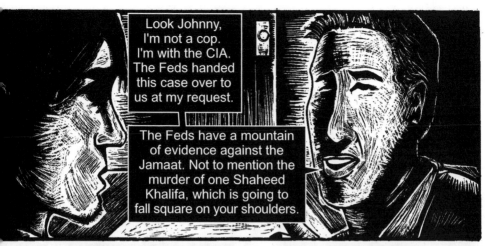

Look Johnny, I'm not a cop. I'm with the CIA. The Feds handed this case over to us at my request.

The Feds have a mountain of evidence against the Jamaat. Not to mention the murder of one Shaheed Khalifa, which is going to fall square on your shoulders.

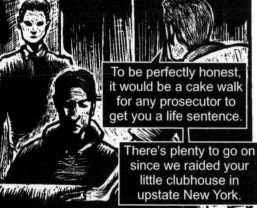

To be perfectly honest, it would be a cake walk for any prosecutor to get you a life sentence.

There's plenty to go on since we raided your little clubhouse in upstate New York.

Do you recognize your friend here? Kazeem Fazil. This is one dangerous guy.

Kazeem trained at a camp in Afghanistan. He intended to send you over there to finish your training.

Ever wonder why he had you learning Pashto?

I'm about to give you a little history lesson in CIA affairs.

Pay attention. This information just might save your ass from an extended trip to Federal prison.

What I'm about to tell you doesn't leave this room. Got me?

Yeah.

You even whisper this information to the wind and I will personally cut your tongue out. Clear?

Y-yes, sir.

The CIA has been funding mujahideen since the Soviet war, that's no secret.

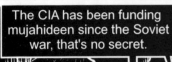

A fundamentalist offshoot of mujahideen are battling Russian backed warlords in Afghanistan. There's an oil-pipeline, well that doesn't concern you...

...They're called the Taliban. The problem is, they're also anti-American. That doesn't matter, we want to keep funding these freedom fighters.

Pakistani intelligence, or the ISI, funnels U.S. guns and money to the Taliban. It's in our best interest to see they control Afghanistan.

Better the Talibs than the Russians or those crazy Iranians.

The Talibs run the training camps. If Iranians or the Russians get out of hand, the Talibs will hold them off.

And the best part is that nobody knows where the support is really coming from.

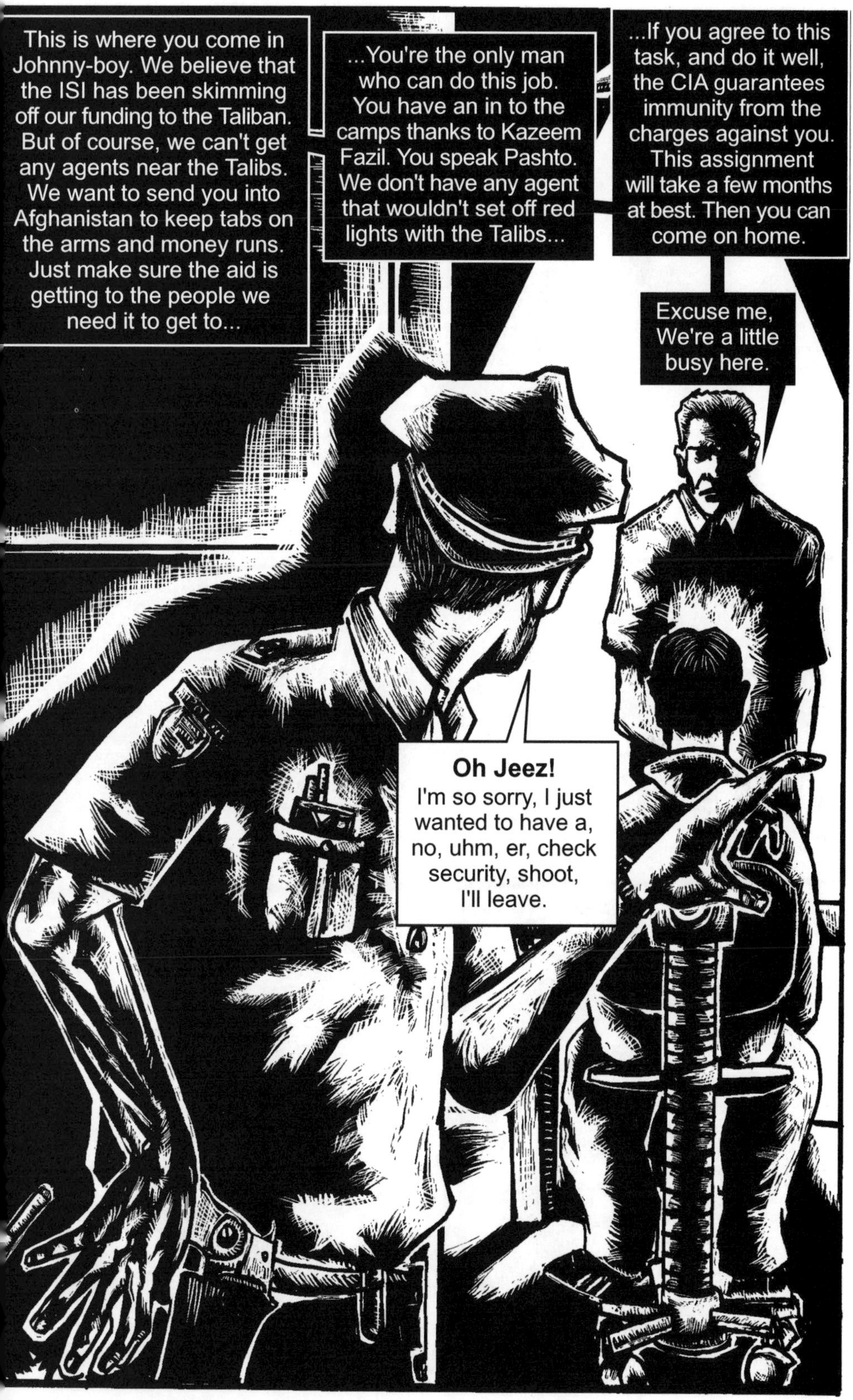
This is where you come in Johnny-boy. We believe that the ISI has been skimming off our funding to the Taliban. But of course, we can't get any agents near the Talibs. We want to send you into Afghanistan to keep tabs on the arms and money runs. Just make sure the aid is getting to the people we need it to get to...
...You're the only man who can do this job. You have an in to the camps thanks to Kazeem Fazil. You speak Pashto. We don't have any agent that wouldn't set off red lights with the Talibs...
...If you agree to this task, and do it well, the CIA guarantees immunity from the charges against you. This assignment will take a few months at best. Then you can come on home.
Excuse me, We're a little busy here.
Oh Jeez! I'm so sorry, I just wanted to have a, no, uhm, er, check security, shoot, I'll leave.

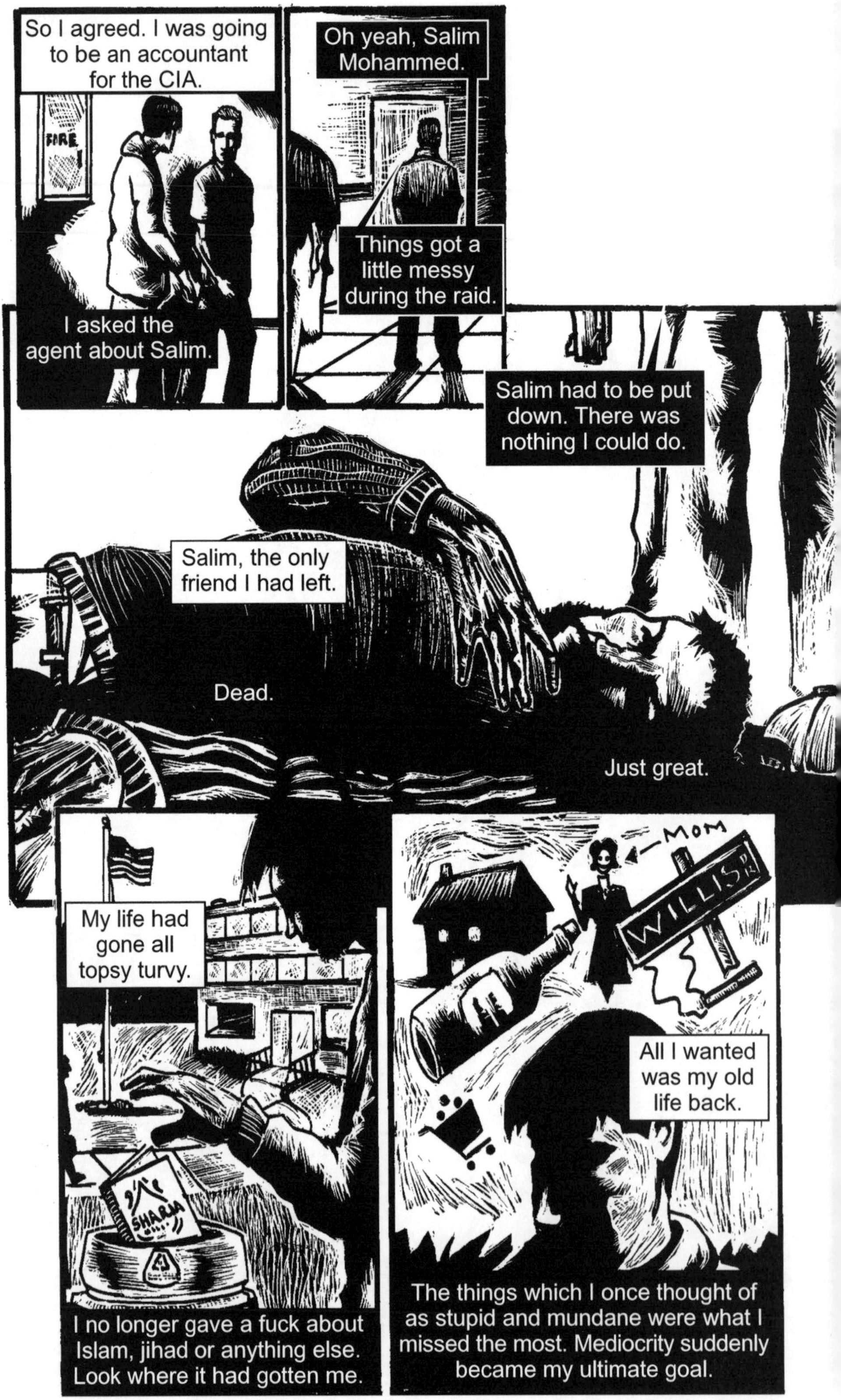
So I agreed. I was going to be an accountant for the CIA.
I asked the agent about Salim.
Oh yeah, Salim Mohammed.
Things got a little messy during the raid.
Salim had to be put down. There was nothing I could do.
Salim, the only friend I had left.
Dead.
Just great.
My life had gone all topsy turvy.
SHARIA
I no longer gave a fuck about Islam, jihad or anything else. Look where it had gotten me.
MOM
WILLIS DR
All I wanted was my old life back.
The things which I once thought of as stupid and mundane were what I missed the most. Mediocrity suddenly became my ultimate goal.

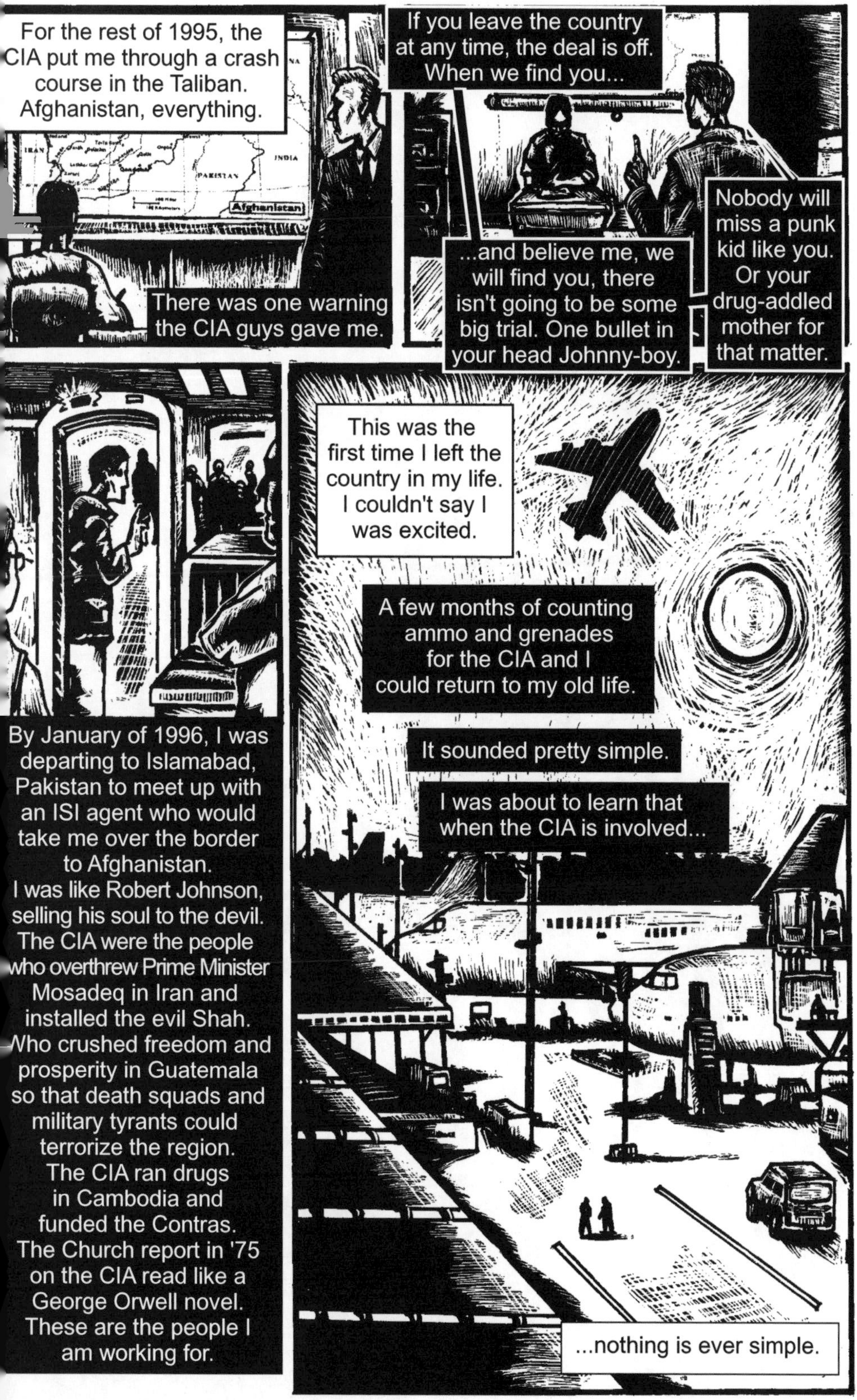
For the rest of 1995, the CIA put me through a crash course in the Taliban. Afghanistan, everything.
INDIA
PAKISTAN
Afghanistan
There was one warning the CIA guys gave me.
If you leave the country at any time, the deal is off. When we find you...
...and believe me, we will find you, there isn't going to be some big trial. One bullet in your head Johnny-boy.
Nobody will miss a punk kid like you. Or your drug-addled mother for that matter.
By January of 1996, I was departing to Islamabad, Pakistan to meet up with an ISI agent who would take me over the border to Afghanistan. I was like Robert Johnson, selling his soul to the devil. The CIA were the people who overthrew Prime Minister Mosadeq in Iran and installed the evil Shah. Who crushed freedom and prosperity in Guatemala so that death squads and military tyrants could terrorize the region. The CIA ran drugs in Cambodia and funded the Contras. The Church report in '75 on the CIA read like a George Orwell novel. These are the people I am working for.
This was the first time I left the country in my life. I couldn't say I was excited.
A few months of counting ammo and grenades for the CIA and I could return to my old life.
It sounded pretty simple.
I was about to learn that when the CIA is involved...
...nothing is ever simple.

AFGHANISTAN

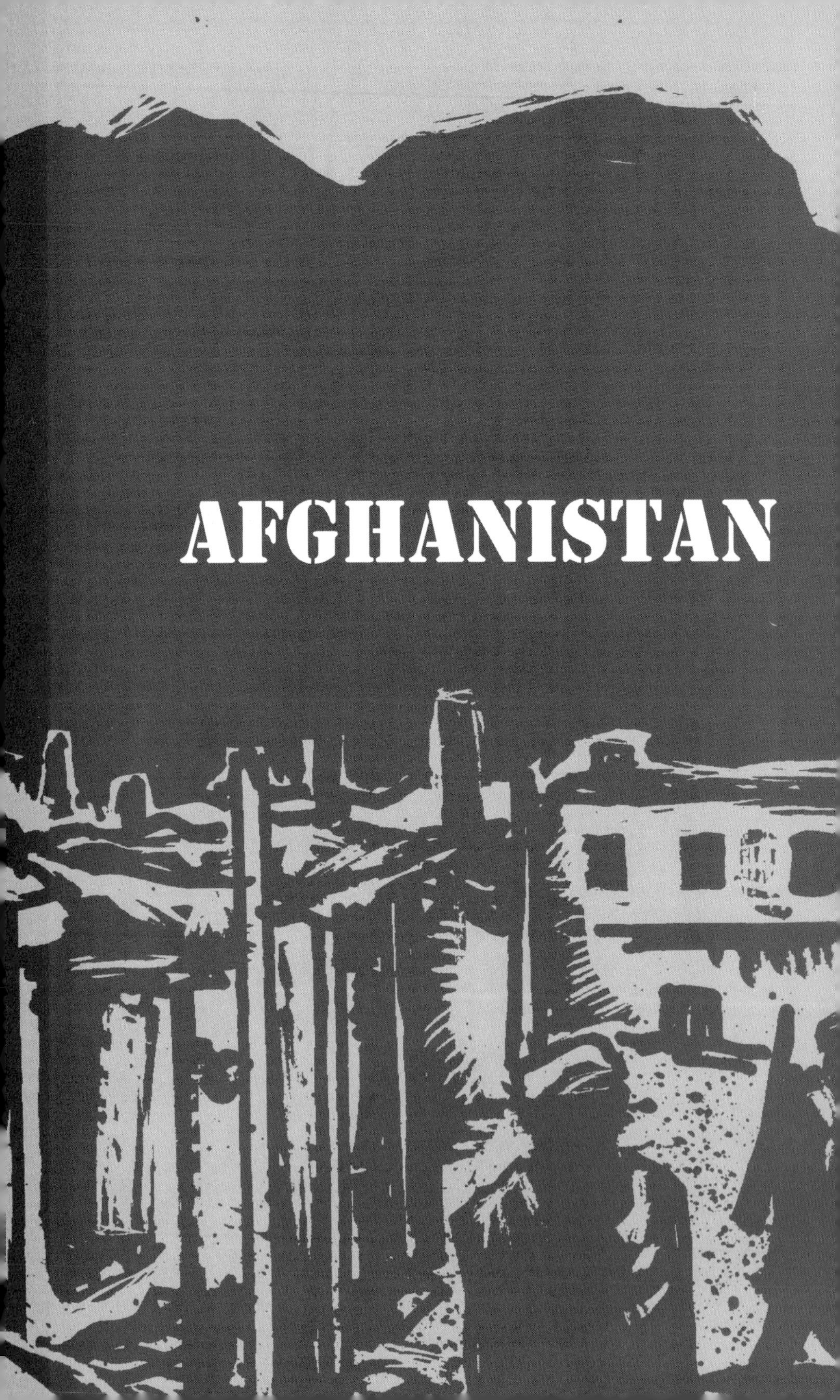

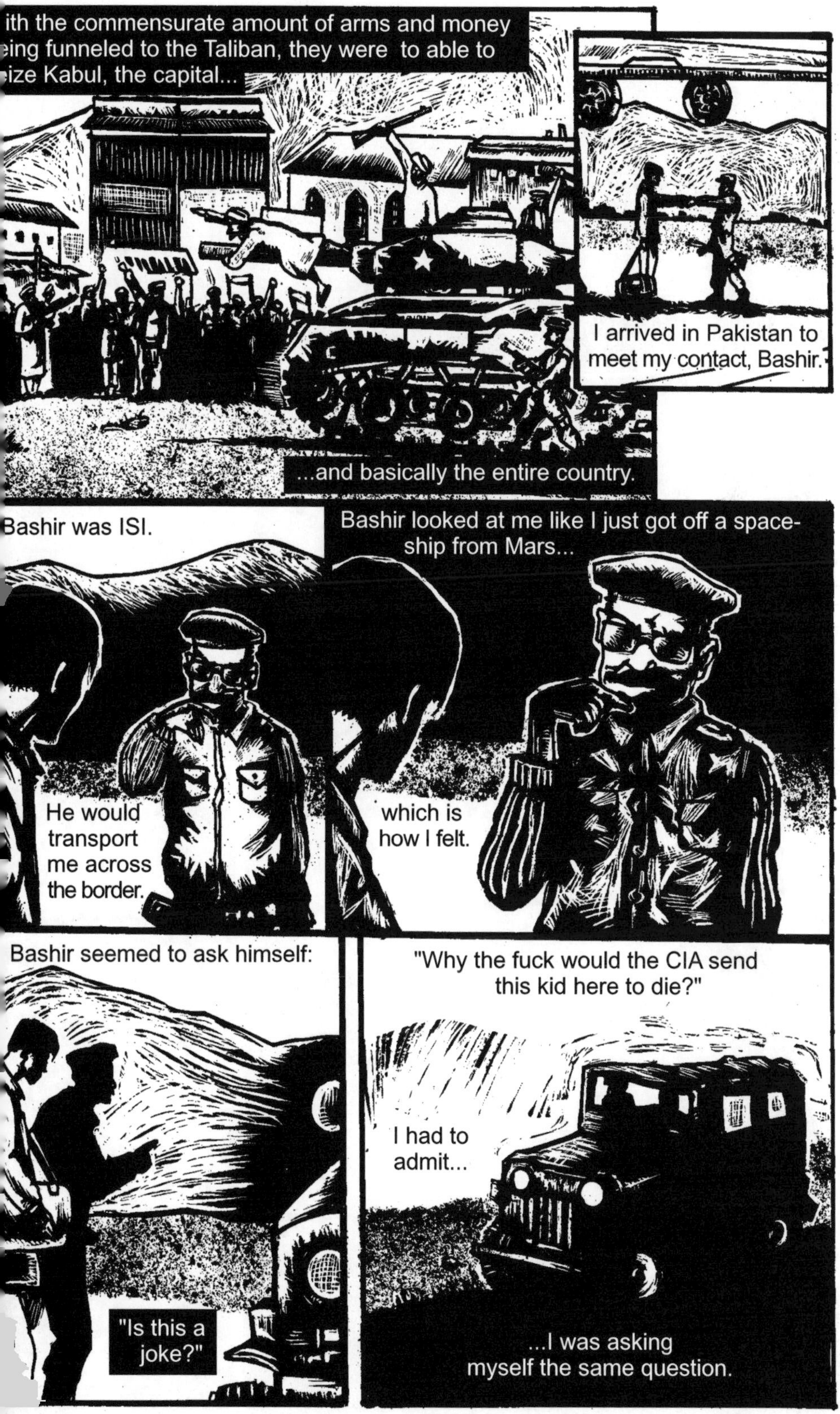
ith the commensurate amount of arms and money
eing funneled to the Taliban, they were to able to
eize Kabul, the capital...
I arrived in Pakistan to meet my contact, Bashir.
...and basically the entire country.
Bashir was ISI.
He would transport me across the border.
Bashir looked at me like I just got off a space-ship from Mars...
which is how I felt.
Bashir seemed to ask himself:
"Is this a joke?"
"Why the fuck would the CIA send this kid here to die?"
I had to admit...
...I was asking myself the same question.

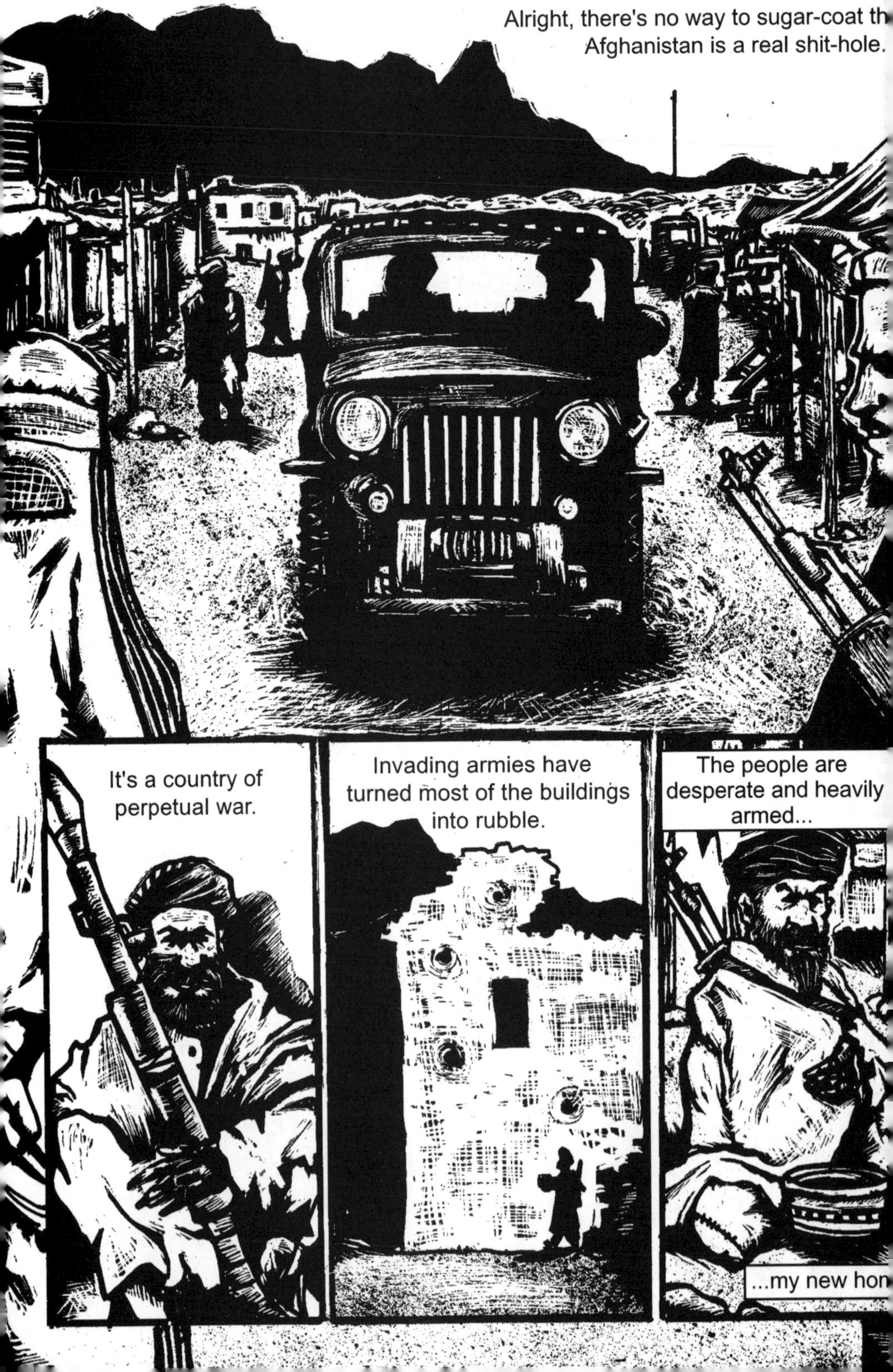
Alright, there's no way to sugar-coat th
Afghanistan is a real shit-hole.
It's a country of perpetual war.
Invading armies have turned most of the buildings into rubble.
The people are desperate and heavily armed...
...my new hon

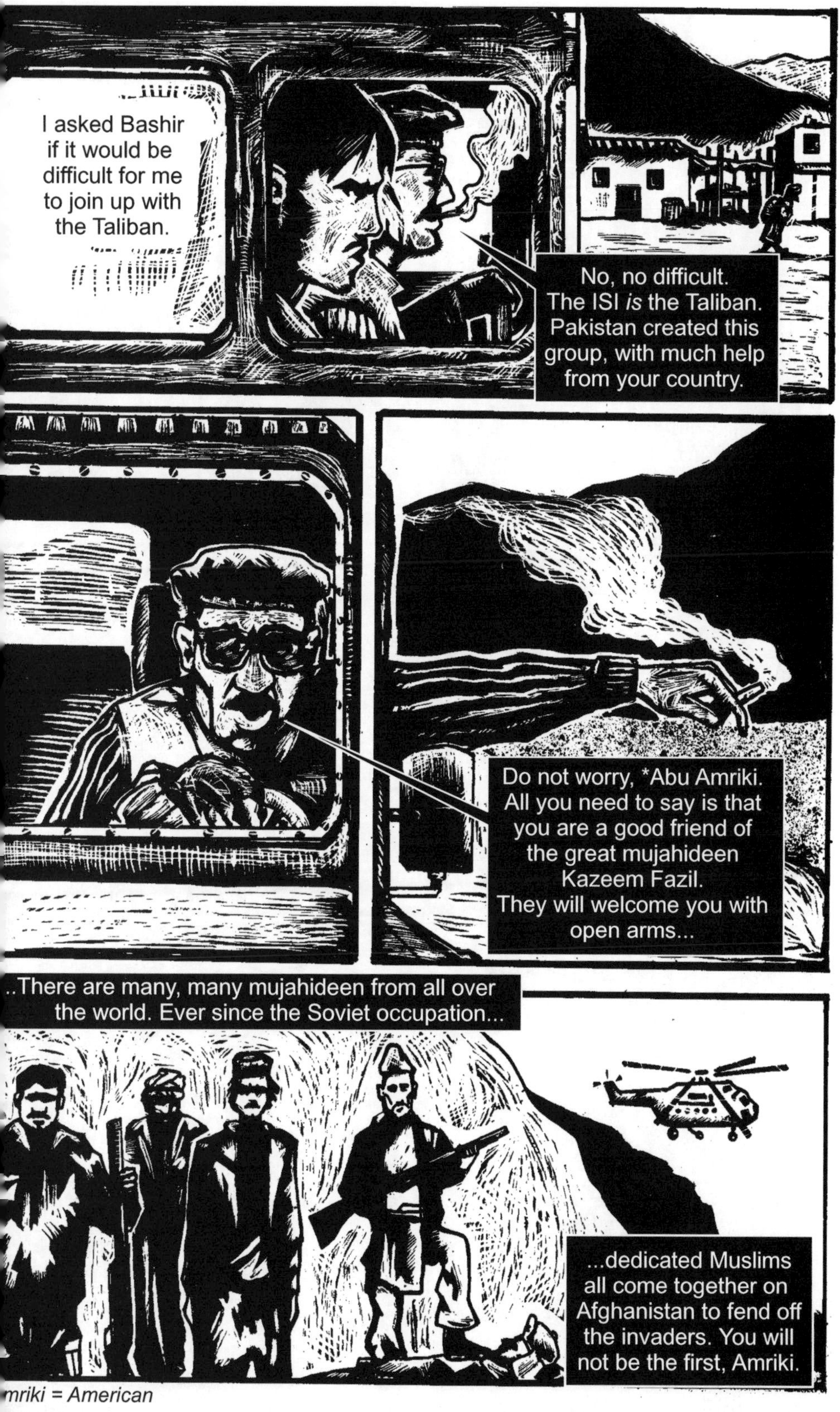
I asked Bashir if it would be difficult for me to join up with the Taliban.
No, no difficult. The ISI *is* the Taliban. Pakistan created this group, with much help from your country.
Do not worry, *Abu Amriki. All you need to say is that you are a good friend of the great mujahideen Kazeem Fazil. They will welcome you with open arms...
..There are many, many mujahideen from all over the world. Ever since the Soviet occupation...
...dedicated Muslims all come together on Afghanistan to fend off the invaders. You will not be the first, Amriki.

mriki = American

The Taliban had just seized Kabul from the ethnic Tajik militia.

The Talibs gain more ground every day.

Most warlords give up their land without even fighting!

It didn't seem like the Talibs needed any more weapons...

...but of course, that wouldn't deter the CIA from sending them.

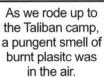

As we rode up to the Taliban camp, a pungent smell of burnt plasitc was in the air.

Video cassettes. Talibs burn western devices.

I thought of the Stooges tape in my bag...

I couldn't let them burn Iggy

But not the western weapons! They keep those.

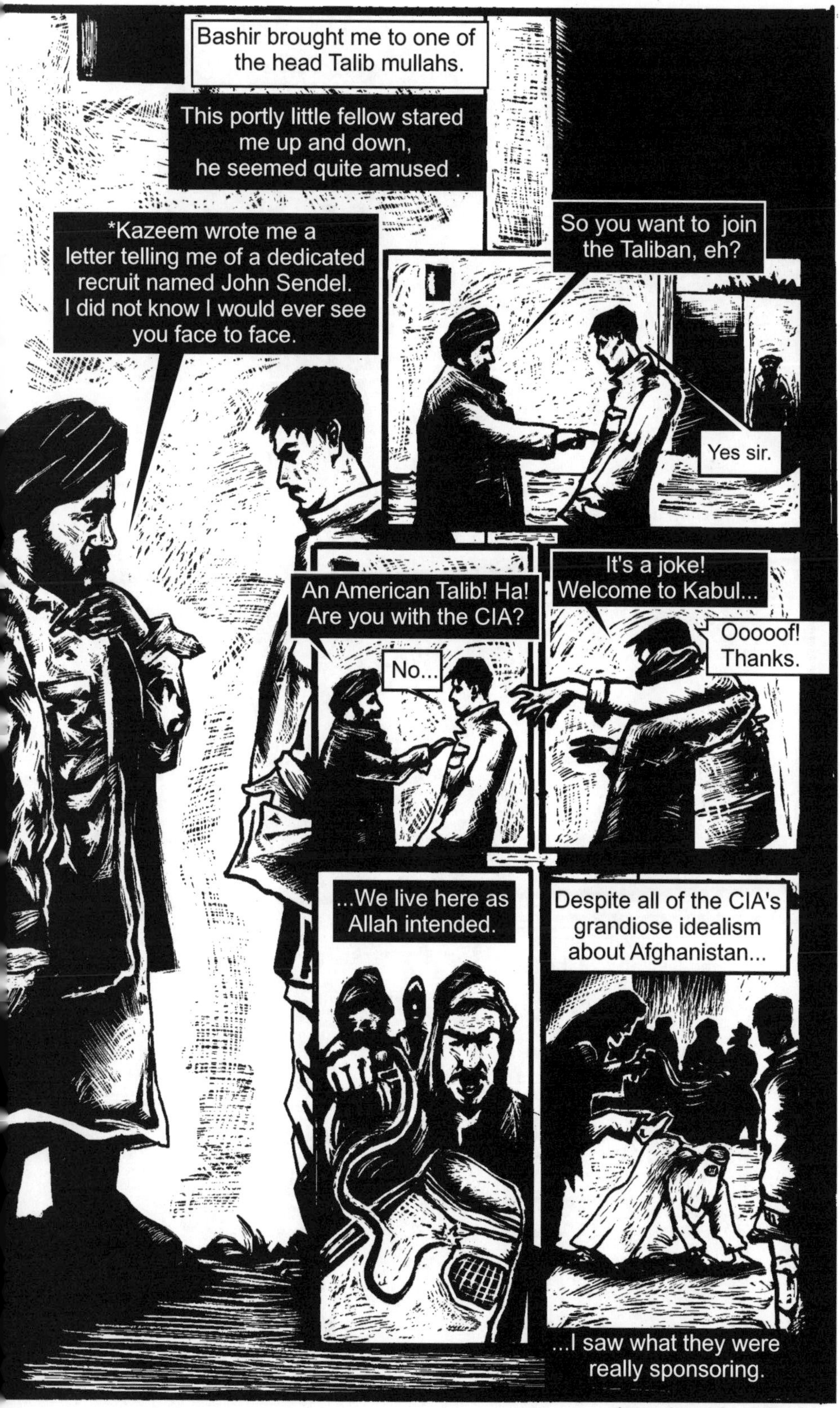
Bashir brought me to one of the head Talib mullahs.
This portly little fellow stared me up and down, he seemed quite amused .
*Kazeem wrote me a letter telling me of a dedicated recruit named John Sendel. I did not know I would ever see you face to face.
So you want to join the Taliban, eh?
Yes sir.
An American Talib! Ha! Are you with the CIA?
No...
It's a joke! Welcome to Kabul...
Ooooof! Thanks.
...We live here as Allah intended.
Despite all of the CIA's grandiose idealism about Afghanistan...
...I saw what they were really sponsoring.

*translated from Pashto

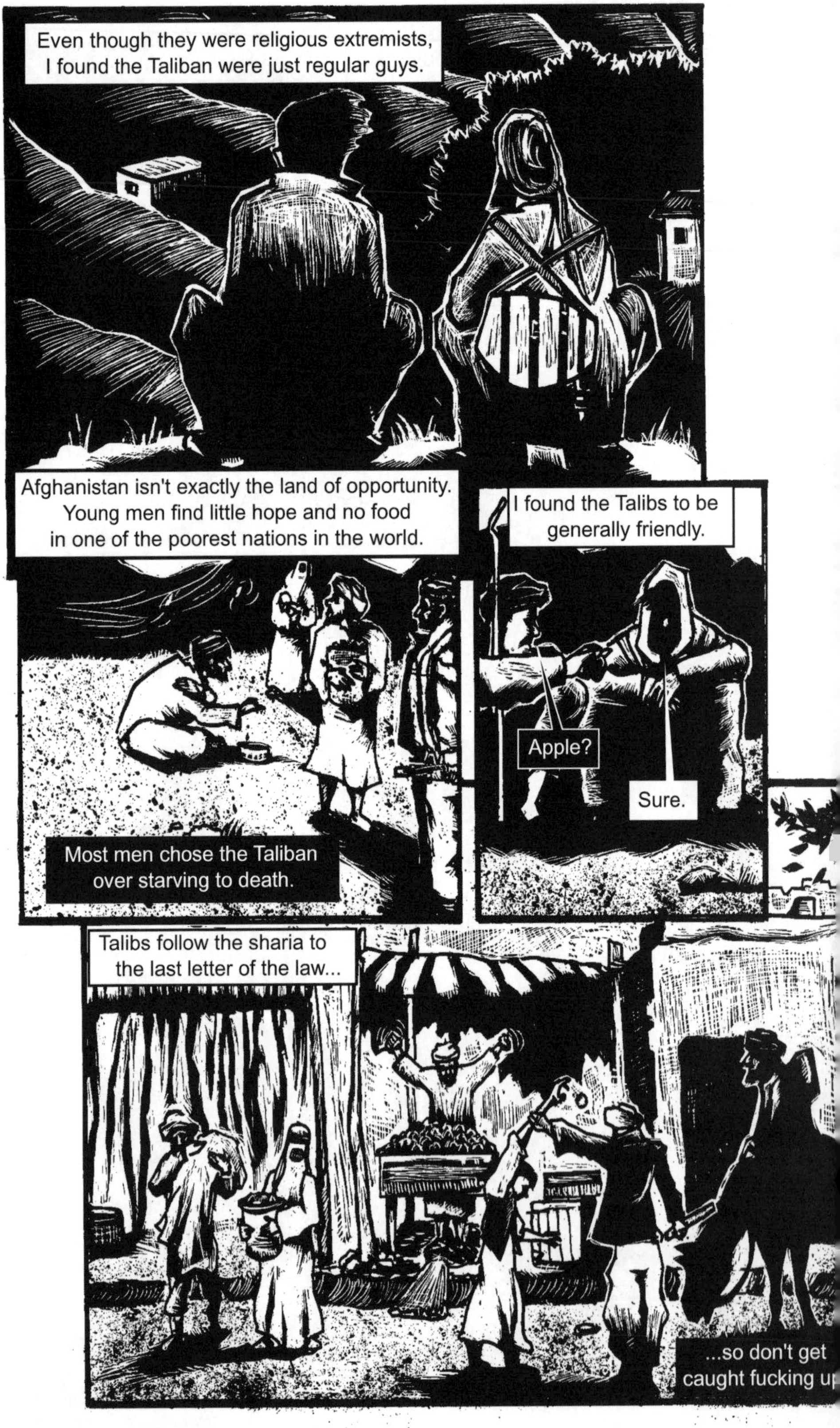
Even though they were religious extremists,
I found the Taliban were just regular guys.
Afghanistan isn't exactly the land of opportunity.
Young men find little hope and no food
in one of the poorest nations in the world.
Most men chose the Taliban
over starving to death.
I found the Talibs to be
generally friendly.
Apple?
Sure.
Talibs follow the sharia to
the last letter of the law...
...so don't get
caught fucking up

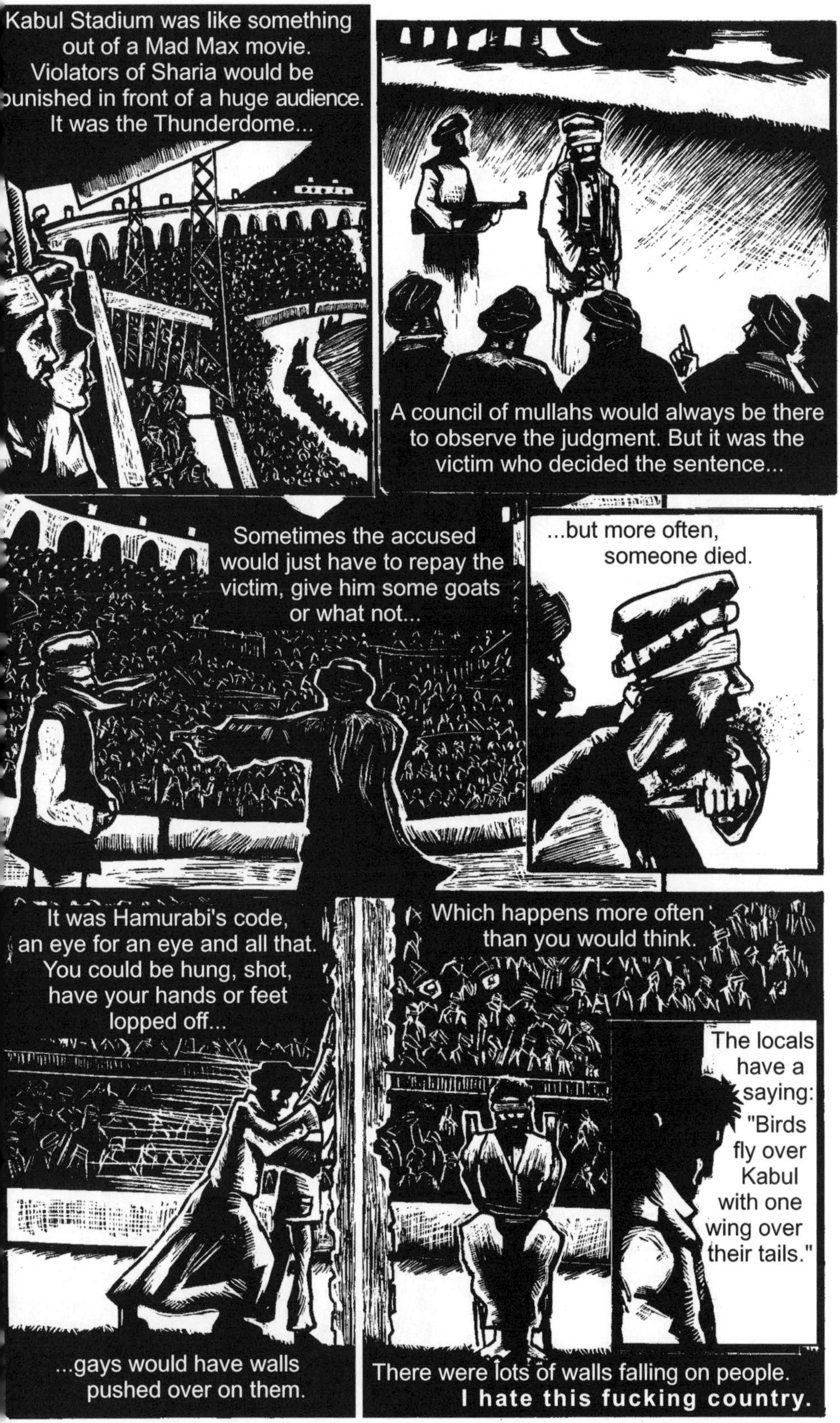
Kabul Stadium was like something out of a Mad Max movie. Violators of Sharia would be punished in front of a huge audience. It was the Thunderdome...
A council of mullahs would always be there to observe the judgment. But it was the victim who decided the sentence...
Sometimes the accused would just have to repay the victim, give him some goats or what not...
...but more often, someone died.
It was Hamurabi's code, an eye for an eye and all that. You could be hung, shot, have your hands or feet lopped off...
...gays would have walls pushed over on them.
Which happens more often than you would think.
The locals have a saying: "Birds fly over Kabul with one wing over their tails."
There were lots of walls falling on people.
I hate this fucking country.

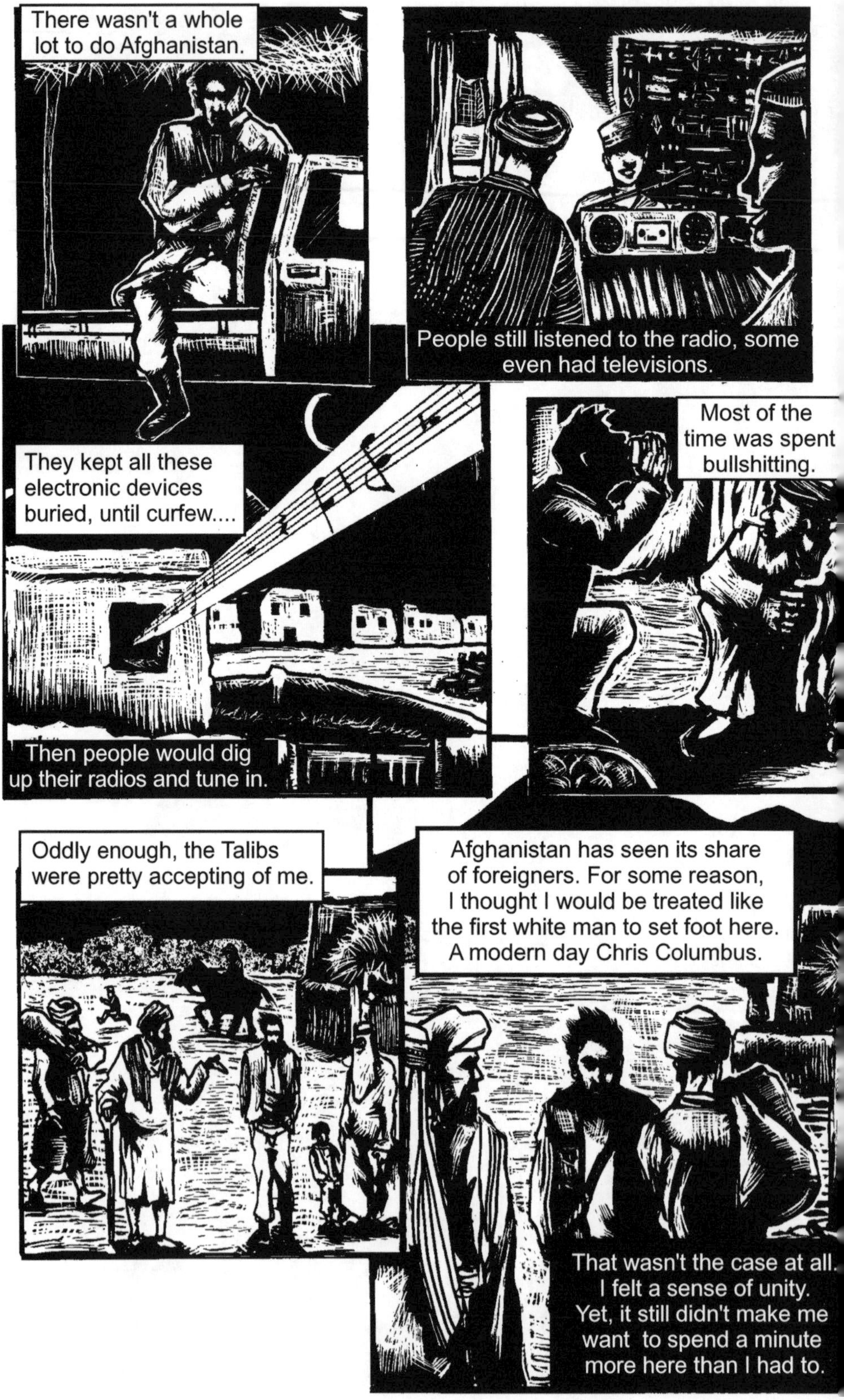

There wasn't a whole lot to do Afghanistan.
People still listened to the radio, some even had televisions.
They kept all these electronic devices buried, until curfew....
Then people would dig up their radios and tune in.
Most of the time was spent bullshitting.
Oddly enough, the Talibs were pretty accepting of me.
Afghanistan has seen its share of foreigners. For some reason, I thought I would be treated like the first white man to set foot here. A modern day Chris Columbus.
That wasn't the case at all. I felt a sense of unity. Yet, it still didn't make me want to spend a minute more here than I had to.

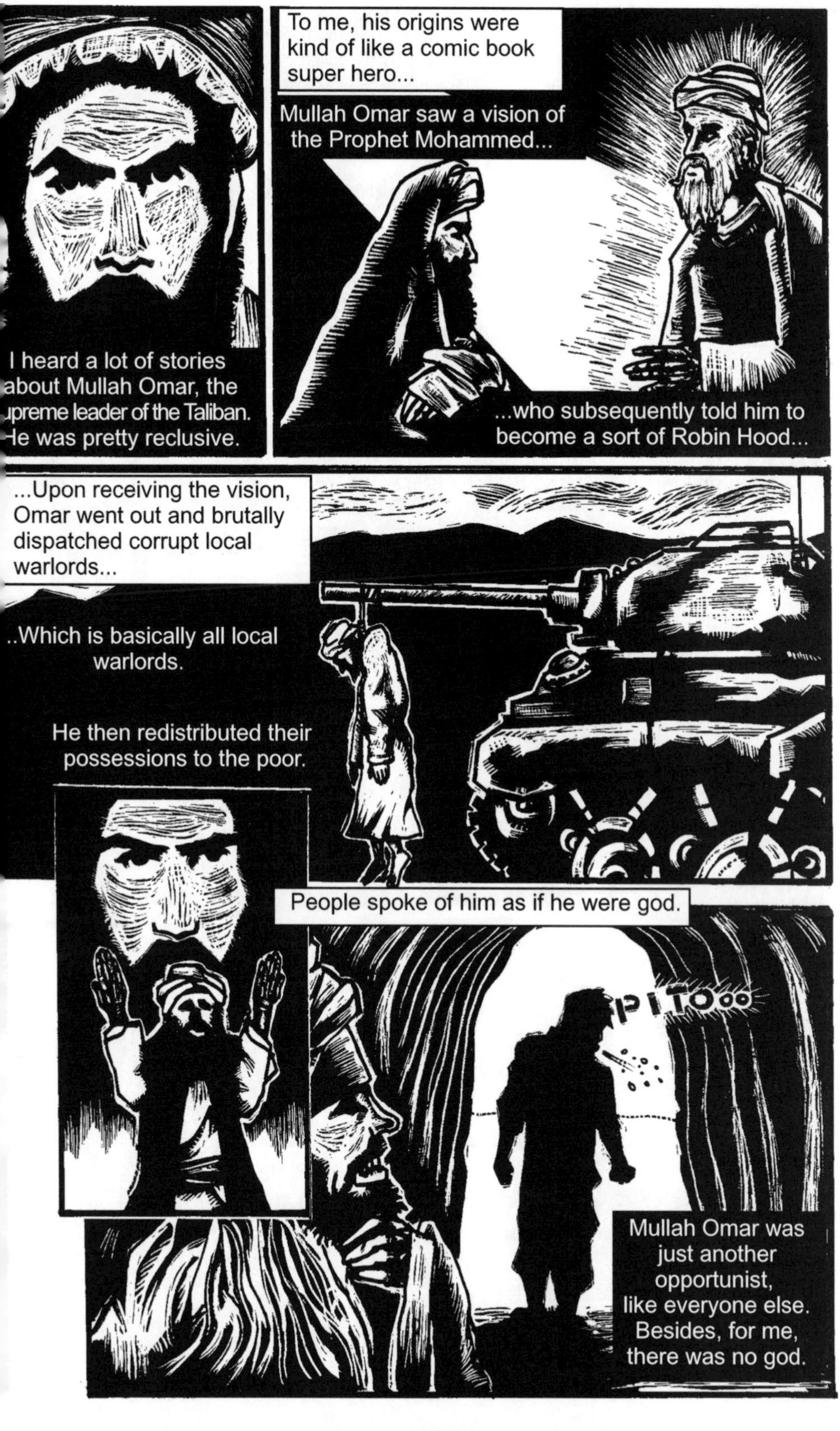
I heard a lot of stories
about Mullah Omar, the
upreme leader of the Taliban.
He was pretty reclusive.
To me, his origins were
kind of like a comic book
super hero...
Mullah Omar saw a vision of
the Prophet Mohammed...
...who subsequently told him to
become a sort of Robin Hood...
...Upon receiving the vision,
Omar went out and brutally
dispatched corrupt local
warlords...
..Which is basically all local
warlords.
He then redistributed their
possessions to the poor.
People spoke of him as if he were god.
PTOoo
Mullah Omar was
just another
opportunist,
like everyone else.
Besides, for me,
there was no god.

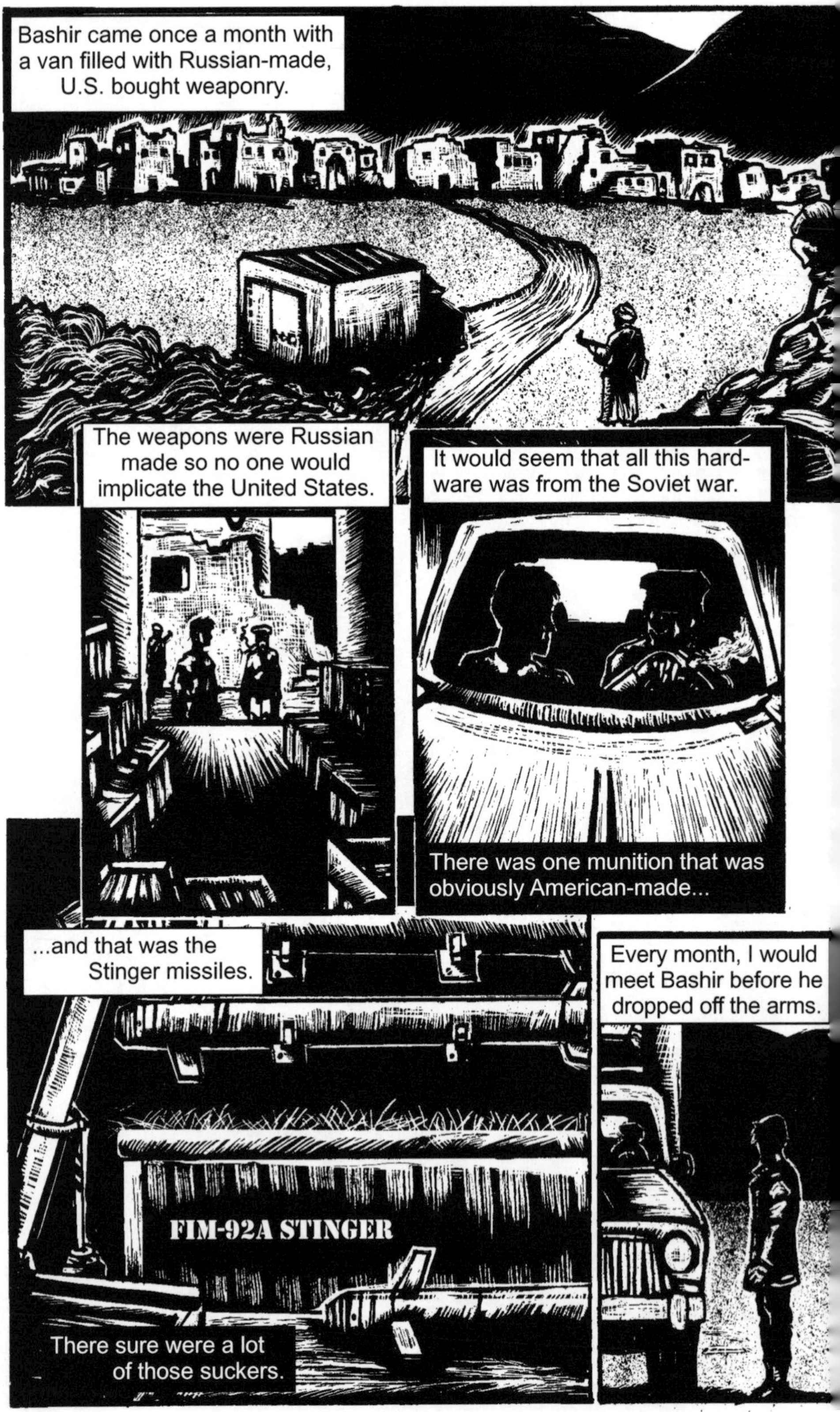
Bashir came once a month with a van filled with Russian-made, U.S. bought weaponry.
The weapons were Russian made so no one would implicate the United States.
It would seem that all this hard-ware was from the Soviet war.
There was one munition that was obviously American-made...
...and that was the Stinger missiles.
FIM-92A STINGER
There sure were a lot of those suckers.
Every month, I would meet Bashir before he dropped off the arms.

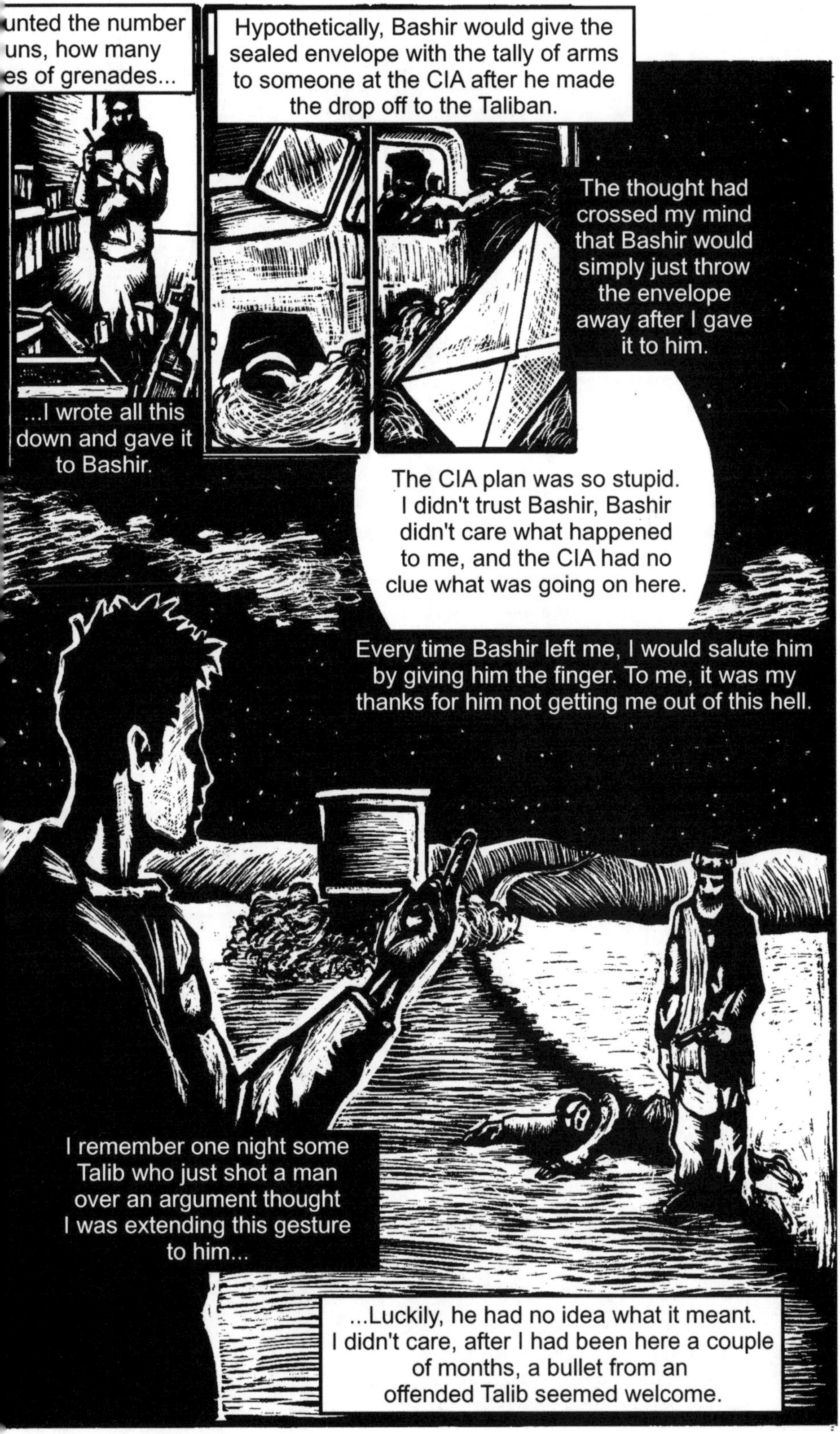
unted the number
uns, how many
es of grenades...
Hypothetically, Bashir would give the sealed envelope with the tally of arms to someone at the CIA after he made the drop off to the Taliban.
The thought had crossed my mind that Bashir would simply just throw the envelope away after I gave it to him.
...I wrote all this down and gave it to Bashir.
The CIA plan was so stupid. I didn't trust Bashir, Bashir didn't care what happened to me, and the CIA had no clue what was going on here.
Every time Bashir left me, I would salute him by giving him the finger. To me, it was my thanks for him not getting me out of this hell.
I remember one night some Talib who just shot a man over an argument thought I was extending this gesture to him...
...Luckily, he had no idea what it meant. I didn't care, after I had been here a couple of months, a bullet from an offended Talib seemed welcome.

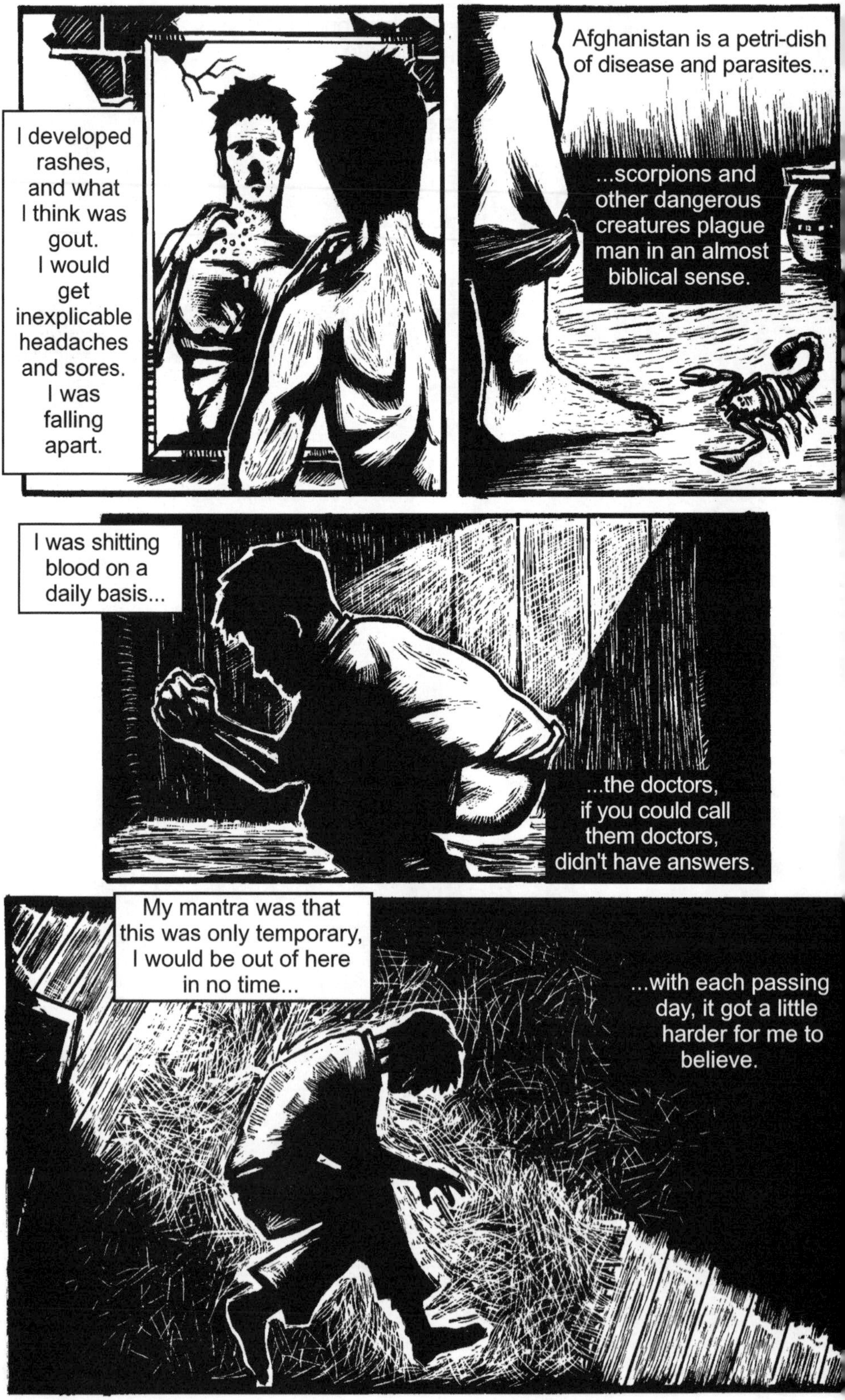

I developed rashes, and what I think was gout. I would get inexplicable headaches and sores. I was falling apart.
Afghanistan is a petri-dish of disease and parasites...
...scorpions and other dangerous creatures plague man in an almost biblical sense.
I was shitting blood on a daily basis...
...the doctors, if you could call them doctors, didn't have answers.
My mantra was that this was only temporary, I would be out of here in no time...
...with each passing day, it got a little harder for me to believe.

maintained my monthly ally of arms with Bashir. What a good little CIA operative I was.

It was the only thing that kept me going.

Hey Amriki, don't forget to count this one.

One day, Bashir would take me with him, I thought. My Pakistani knight in shining armor.

Each time he came, it was always the same, "Sorry Amriki, no word yet."

October

November

December

January

February

March

The arms shipments came less frequently. I would wait months in between visits from Bashir. This was a good sign. I thought that it meant that aid was getting cut off, and that for a job well done a ticket home was imminent.

On one of Bashir's sporadic arms drop offs, I asked him what was going on.

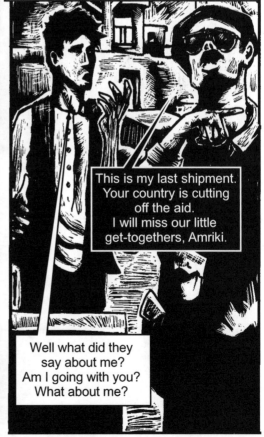

This is my last shipment. Your country is cutting off the aid. I will miss our little get-togethers, Amriki.

Well what did they say about me? Am I going with you? What about me?

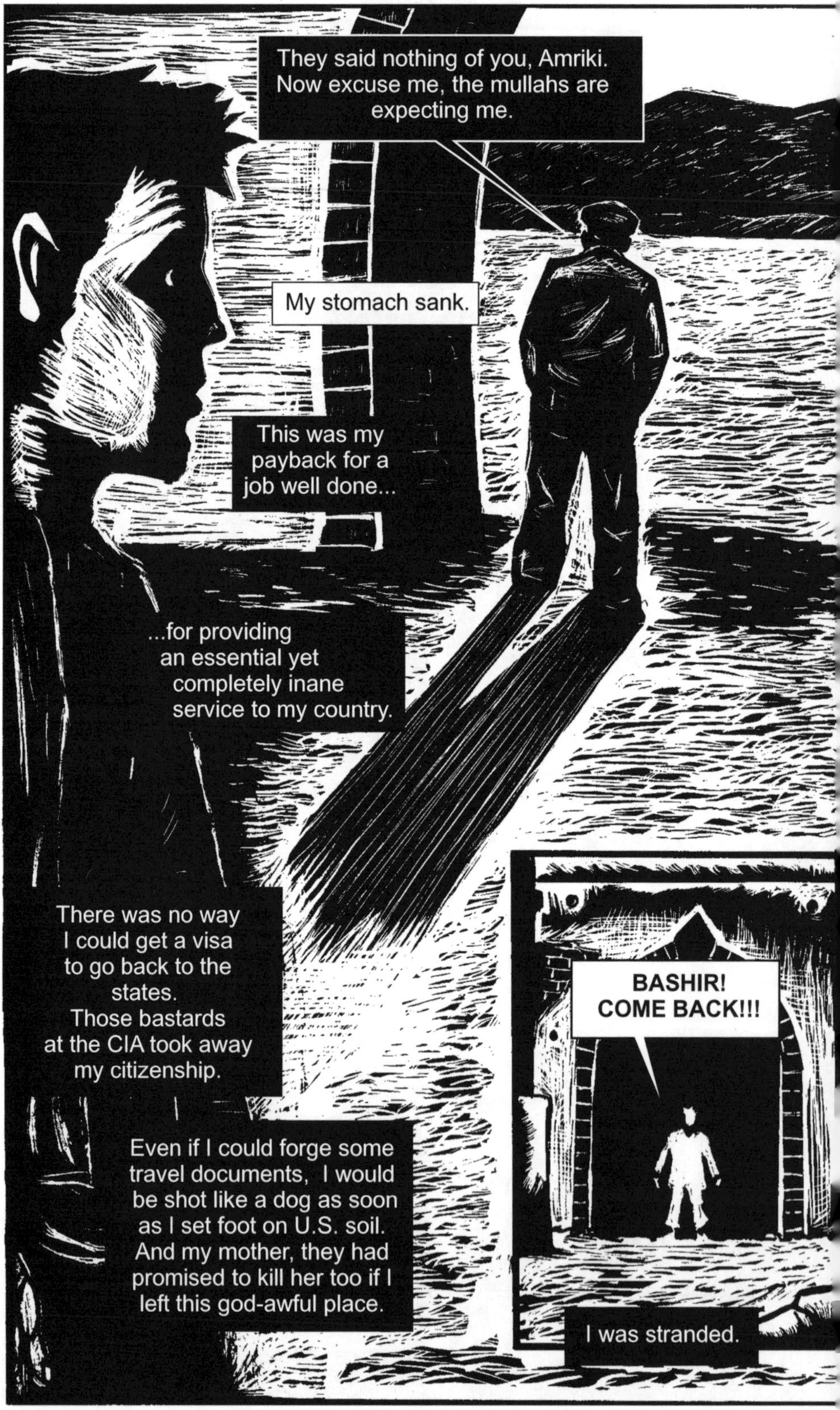

They said nothing of you, Amriki. Now excuse me, the mullahs are expecting me.
My stomach sank.
This was my payback for a job well done...
...for providing an essential yet completely inane service to my country.
There was no way I could get a visa to go back to the states. Those bastards at the CIA took away my citizenship.
Even if I could forge some travel documents, I would be shot like a dog as soon as I set foot on U.S. soil. And my mother, they had promised to kill her too if I left this god-awful place.
BASHIR! COME BACK!!!
I was stranded.

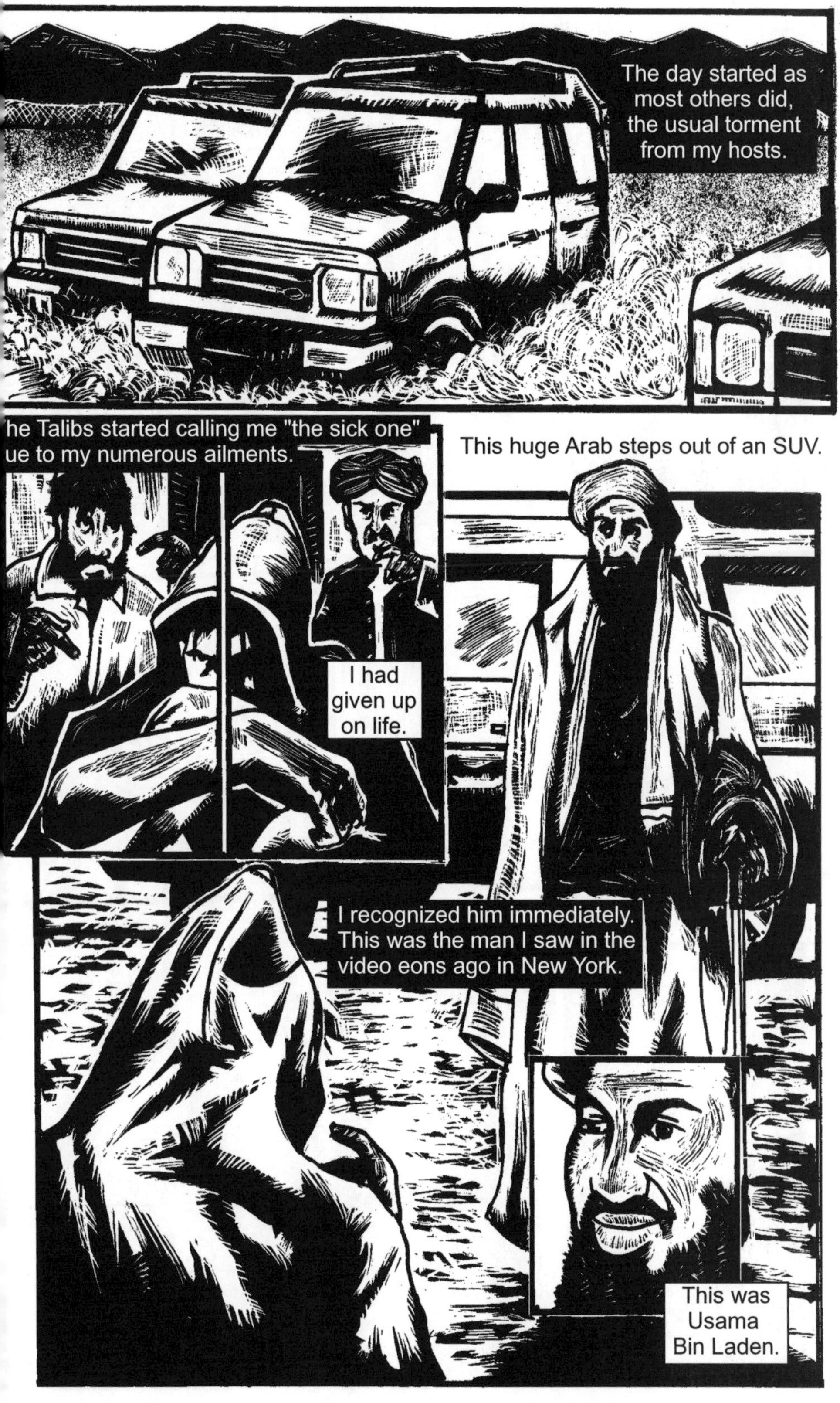
The day started as most others did, the usual torment from my hosts.
he Talibs started calling me "the sick one" ue to my numerous ailments.
I had given up on life.
This huge Arab steps out of an SUV.
I recognized him immediately. This was the man I saw in the video eons ago in New York.
This was Usama Bin Laden.

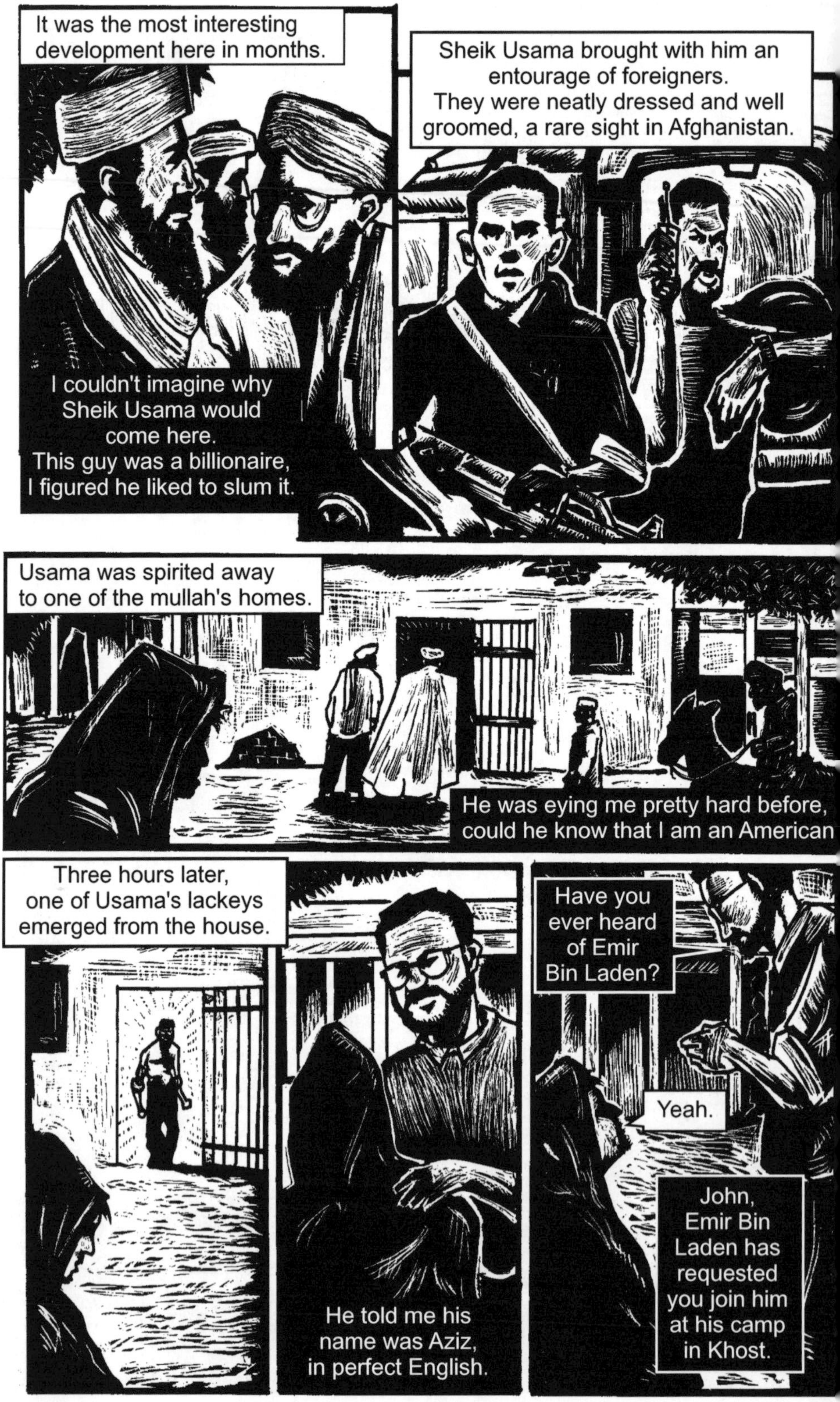

It was the most interesting development here in months.
I couldn't imagine why Sheik Usama would come here. This guy was a billionaire, I figured he liked to slum it.
Sheik Usama brought with him an entourage of foreigners. They were neatly dressed and well groomed, a rare sight in Afghanistan.
Usama was spirited away to one of the mullah's homes.
He was eying me pretty hard before, could he know that I am an American
Three hours later, one of Usama's lackeys emerged from the house.
He told me his name was Aziz, in perfect English.
Have you ever heard of Emir Bin Laden?
Yeah.
John, Emir Bin Laden has requested you join him at his camp in Khost.

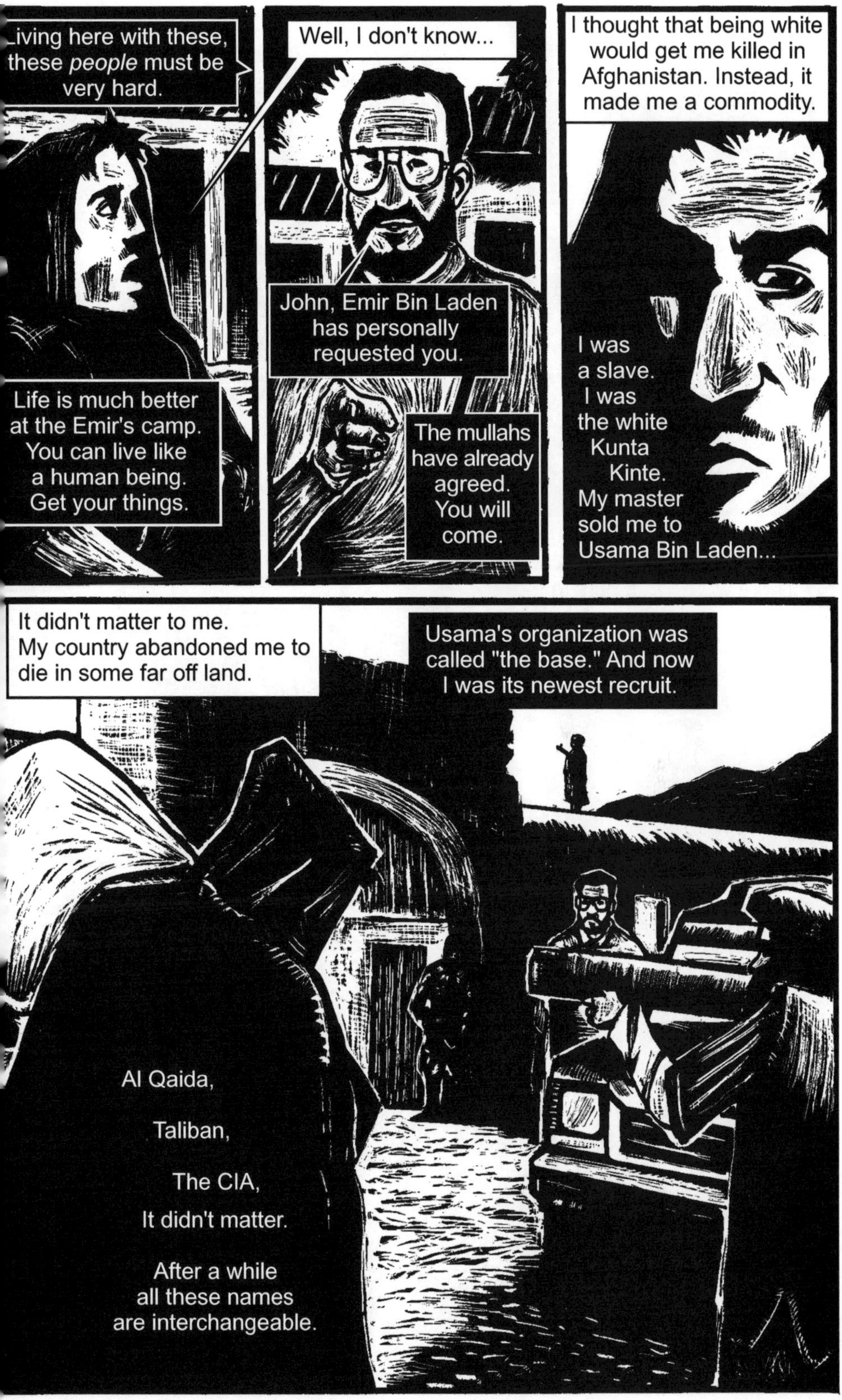
Living here with these, these *people* must be very hard.
Life is much better at the Emir's camp. You can live like a human being. Get your things.
Well, I don't know...
John, Emir Bin Laden has personally requested you.
The mullahs have already agreed. You will come.
I thought that being white would get me killed in Afghanistan. Instead, it made me a commodity.
I was a slave. I was the white Kunta Kinte. My master sold me to Usama Bin Laden...
It didn't matter to me. My country abandoned me to die in some far off land.
Usama's organization was called "the base." And now I was its newest recruit.
Al Qaida,
Taliban,
The CIA,
It didn't matter.
After a while all these names are interchangeable.

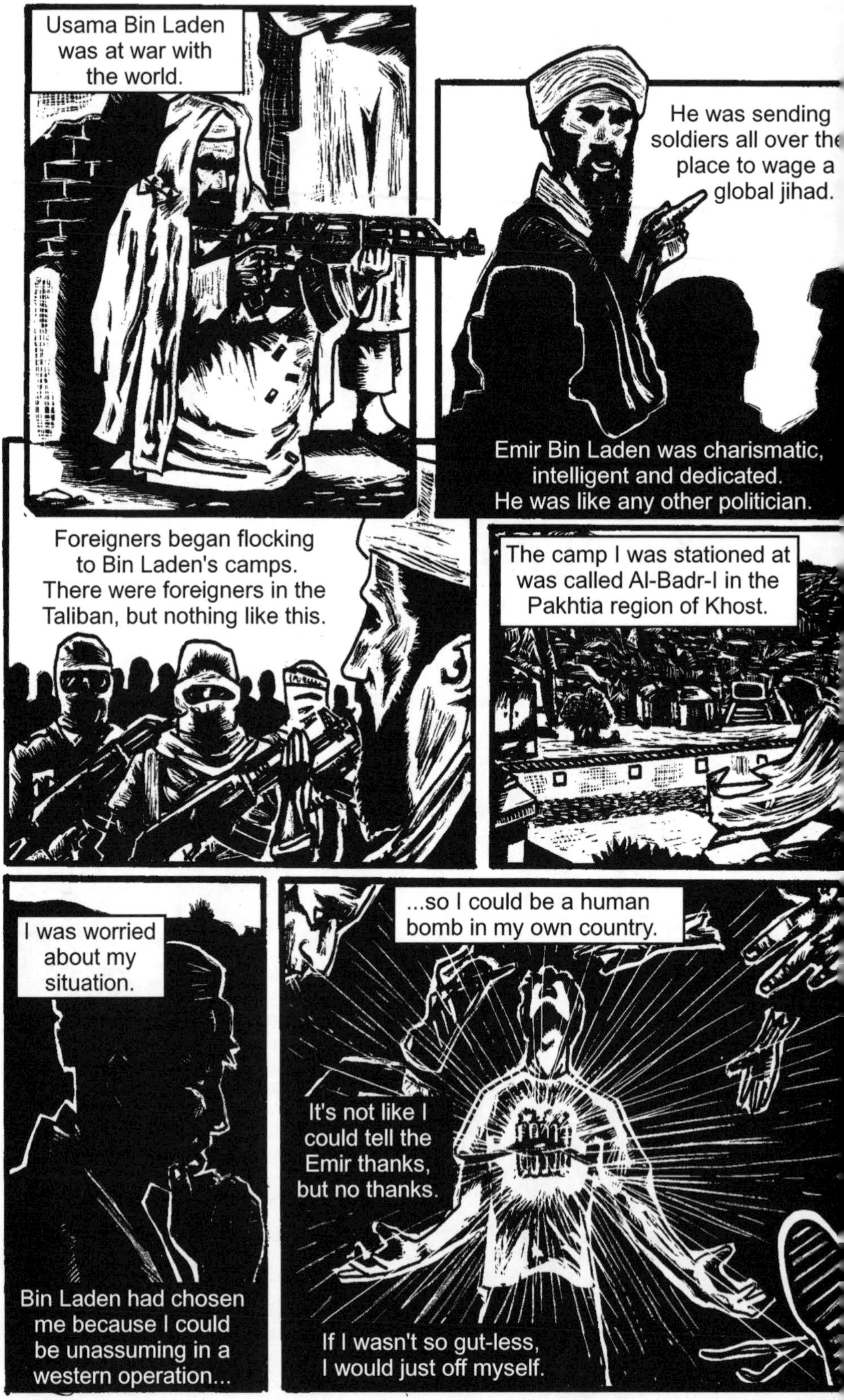
Usama Bin Laden was at war with the world.
He was sending soldiers all over the place to wage a global jihad.
Emir Bin Laden was charismatic, intelligent and dedicated. He was like any other politician.
Foreigners began flocking to Bin Laden's camps. There were foreigners in the Taliban, but nothing like this.
The camp I was stationed at was called Al-Badr-I in the Pakhtia region of Khost.
I was worried about my situation.
Bin Laden had chosen me because I could be unassuming in a western operation...
...so I could be a human bomb in my own country.
It's not like I could tell the Emir thanks, but no thanks.
If I wasn't so gut-less, I would just off myself.

I decided to keep a journal of my time at Al-Badr-I. If someone were to catch me writing in a diary, I would be killed for sure. I imagine death couldn't be much worse than the conditions I am already in.

y 23rd, 1998   Emir Bin Laden summoned for me today. He old me that I was a promising mujahideen and hat he had a "special assignment" for me. A shaheed ission, that means no return ticket. I didn't have o hear anymore. I'm through with being a pawn...

... I immediately went out to the rifle range nd fired a 62mm slug. into my right calf. It's painful as hell, but it will keep me alive.

June 5th, 1998   Due to my medical ondition, I'm of very little use here. Gangrene has set in on my bullet wound. The doctor's only answer was to chop off my eg. I told him, "Fuck that" n English, which he didn't nderstand. I'm trying to keep myself intact. For what reason? I don't know.
    The good news is I'm getting ium for the pain, it's a pasty ush you roll into a ball and smoke.

It makes life just tolerable enough to keep on living...

My new job is to take care of the falcons that are used for communicating with ground troops. Emir Bin Laden is paranoid and doesn't trust modern communications. I strap radio transmitters onto the legs of the falcons and send them off.

Everyone shuns me here. I am a lame, whiteboy from the enemy's country. My only friends are the falcons. I named one 'Salim.' I pray to

god that I don't believe in that Salim isn't shot by some yahoo Talib everytime I send him out. Salim is all I have left.

August 7th, 1998: Much celebrating today as one of the Emir's missions was successful. Twin bombings of the U.S. embassies in Kenya and Tanzania. We troops never ear of what's planned until it's completed. My time is consumed with taking care of he falcons and smoking opium.

Drugs are, of course, forbidden,

but since I was chosen by Bin Laden, no one bothers me. The Talibs I once stayed with tell me that Bin Laden is wearing his welcome thin. Mullah Omar distrusts Bin Laden and wants to turn him over to the Saudis. Good, I told them, fuck'em.

<u>August 20th, 1998:</u>

The U.S. struck back today, bombing ny former living quarters into ubble. Luckily, the ISI had tipped off Bin Laden, and we were able to move nearly everyone out in time. Mullah Omar loves Emir Bin Laden mow that the U.S. is bombing the countryside. He issued a statement saying that the "Great Satan" will never take the Emir from Afghanistan. The U.S. could

have been rid-of Bin Laden forever if not for their heavy trigger finger.

September 11th, 1998

I had to abandon writing in my journal, so I memorized this last entry.
One of the Qaida lieutenants was on to me.
Paranoia amongst the troops is even worse since the American bombing.

I'm no Anne Frank and a journal is not something I want to die over.

Mullah Omar has fully united the Taliban and Bin Laden's Al Qaida.
All of the American weapons, as well as millions of dollars are at the full disposal of Emir Bin Laden.
Good God, what was the CIA thinking?
The Emir has told us troops that America will pay for its treachery.
I don't think he's kidding.

In other matters, I searched through the rubble of Al-Badr-I for my bird, Salim.
I buried him in a shallow grave near the remnants of the camp.

There's nothing left for me.

Most of the troops are relocating to the nearby mountains bordering Pakistan.

I am with a smaller division that will help
rebuild the village hit in the Khost bombing.

The situation here is spiraling out of control, I foresee the worst.
Bin Laden now has the firepower, money and followers to bring the war right to the doorsteps of every single American.

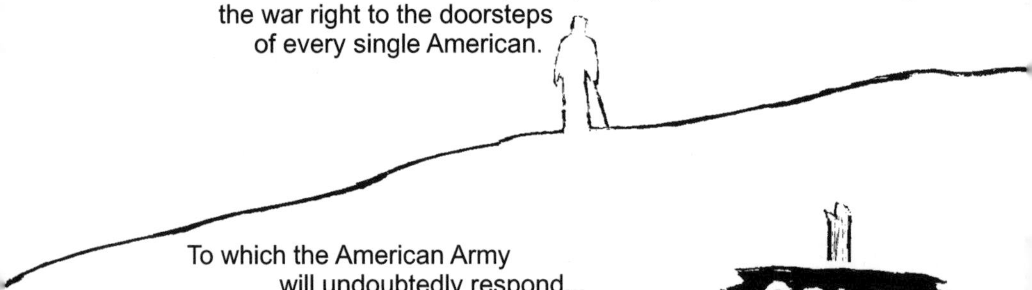

To which the American Army
will undoubtedly respond...

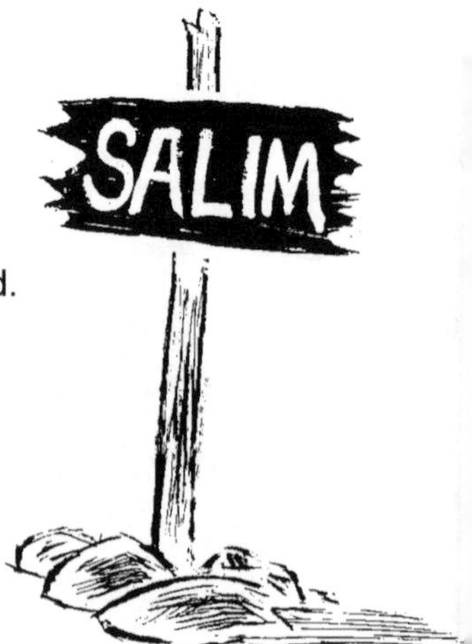
SALIM

Soon we will all be dead.

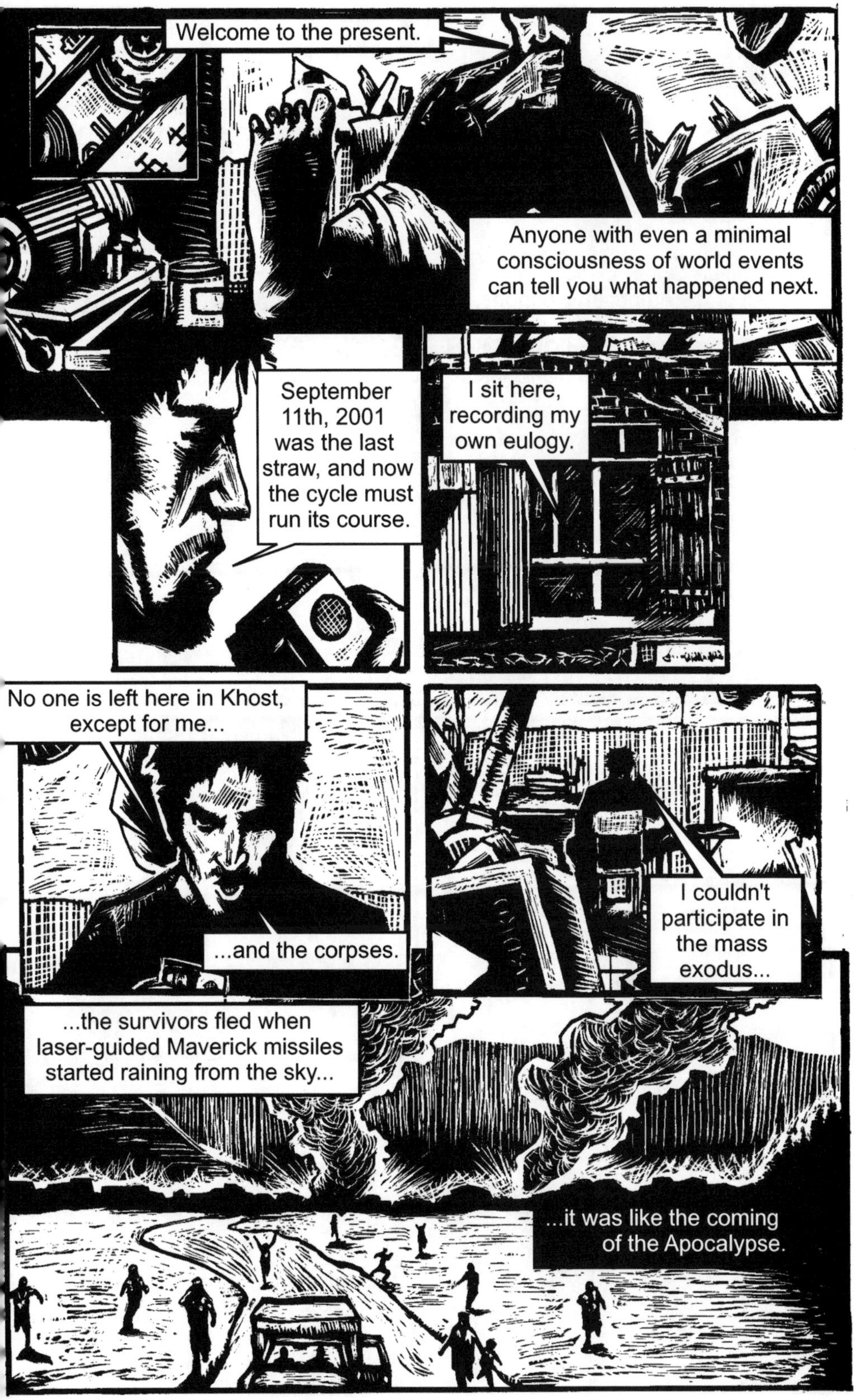
Welcome to the present.
Anyone with even a minimal consciousness of world events can tell you what happened next.
September 11th, 2001 was the last straw, and now the cycle must run its course.
I sit here, recording my own eulogy.
No one is left here in Khost, except for me...
...and the corpses.
I couldn't participate in the mass exodus...
...the survivors fled when laser-guided Maverick missiles started raining from the sky...
...it was like the coming of the Apocalypse.

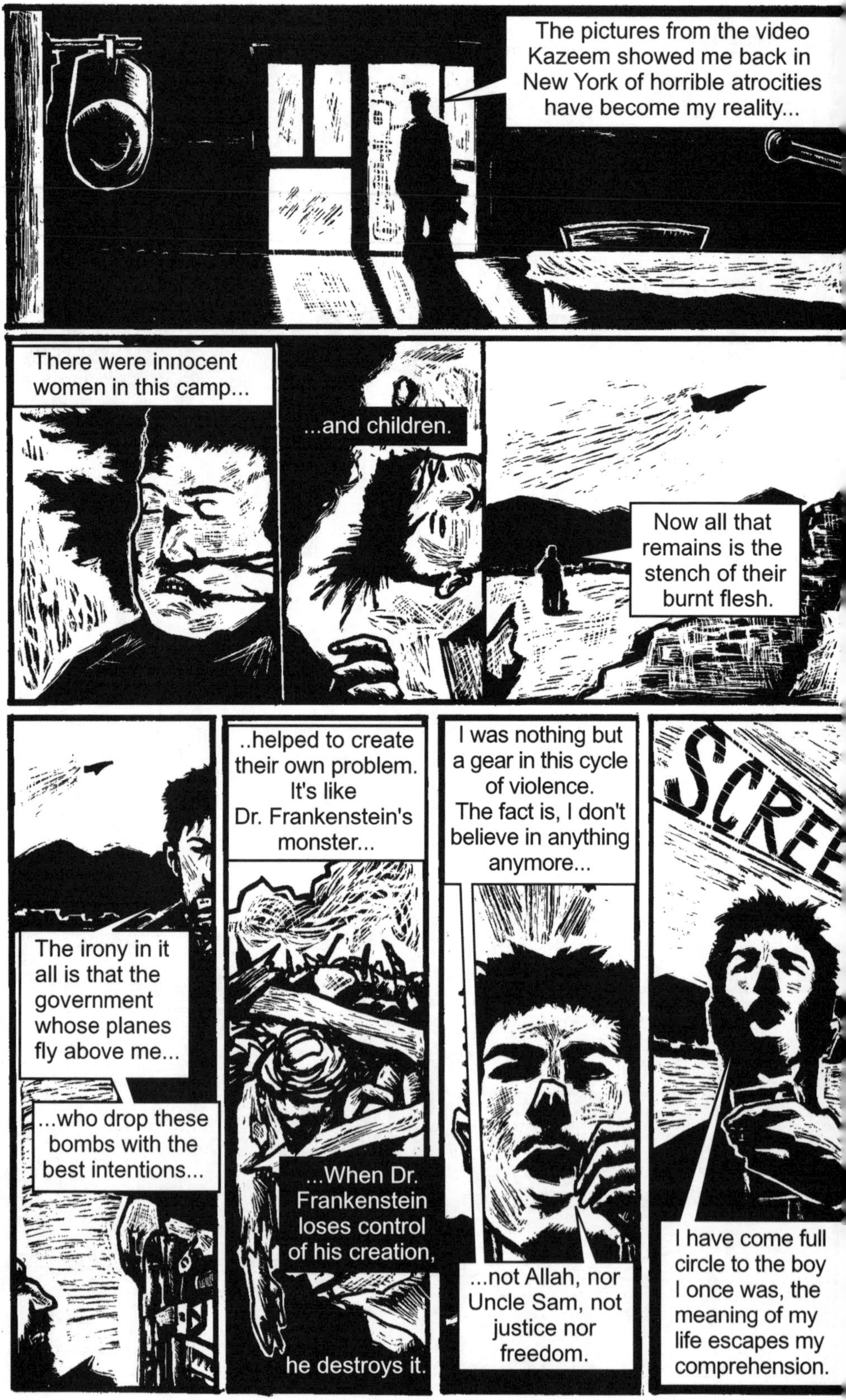

The pictures from the video Kazeem showed me back in New York of horrible atrocities have become my reality...
There were innocent women in this camp...
...and children.
Now all that remains is the stench of their burnt flesh.
The irony in it all is that the government whose planes fly above me...
...who drop these bombs with the best intentions...
..helped to create their own problem. It's like Dr. Frankenstein's monster...
...When Dr. Frankenstein loses control of his creation,
he destroys it.
I was nothing but a gear in this cycle of violence. The fact is, I don't believe in anything anymore...
...not Allah, nor Uncle Sam, not justice nor freedom.
SCREE
I have come full circle to the boy I once was, the meaning of my life escapes my comprehension.

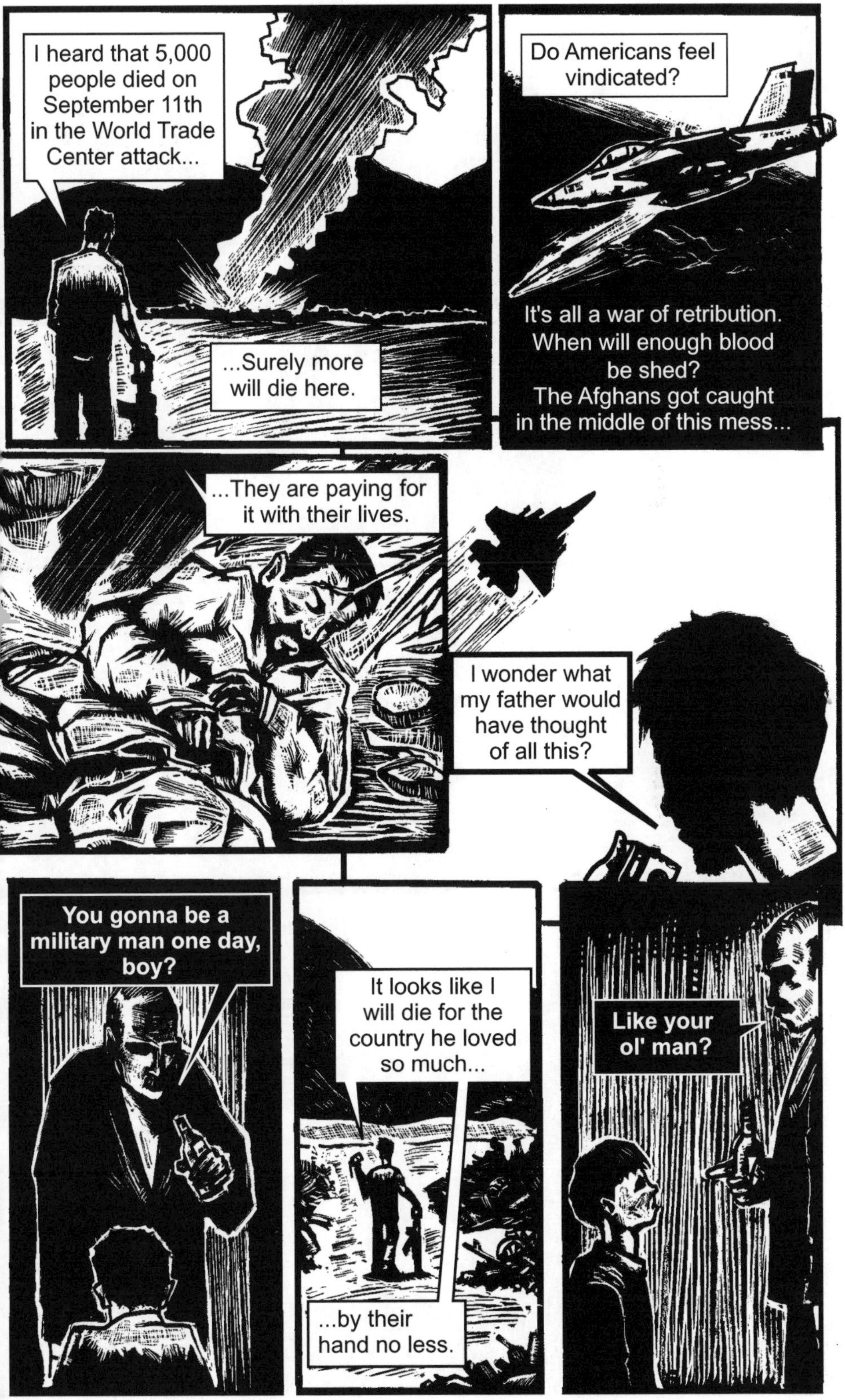
I heard that 5,000 people died on September 11th in the World Trade Center attack...
...Surely more will die here.
Do Americans feel vindicated?
It's all a war of retribution. When will enough blood be shed? The Afghans got caught in the middle of this mess...
...They are paying for it with their lives.
I wonder what my father would have thought of all this?
You gonna be a military man one day, boy?
It looks like I will die for the country he loved so much...
...by their hand no less.
Like your ol' man?

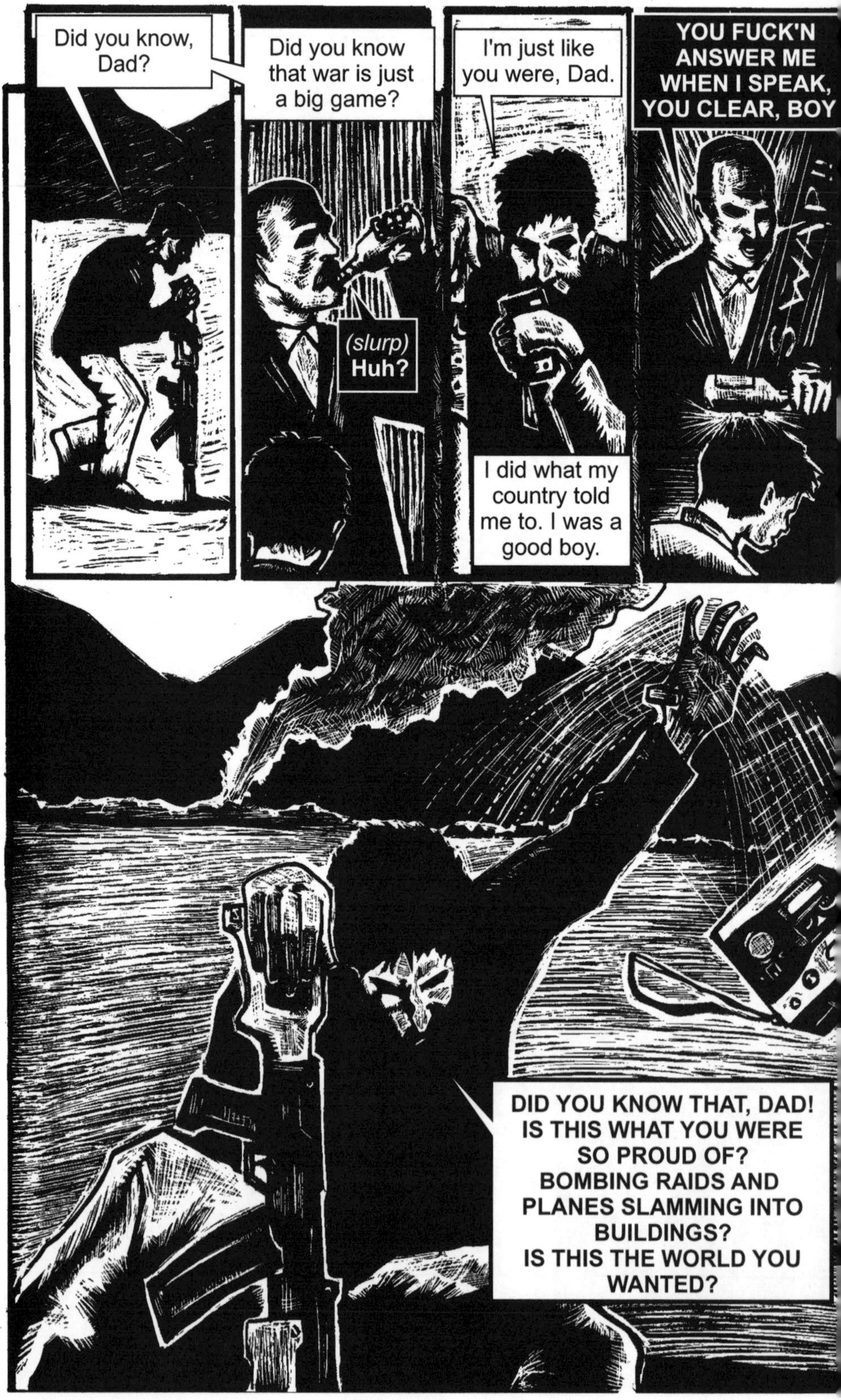

Did you know, Dad?
Did you know that war is just a big game?
(slurp) Huh?
I'm just like you were, Dad.
I did what my country told me to. I was a good boy.
YOU FUCK'N ANSWER ME WHEN I SPEAK, YOU CLEAR, BOY
DID YOU KNOW THAT, DAD! IS THIS WHAT YOU WERE SO PROUD OF? BOMBING RAIDS AND PLANES SLAMMING INTO BUILDINGS? IS THIS THE WORLD YOU WANTED?

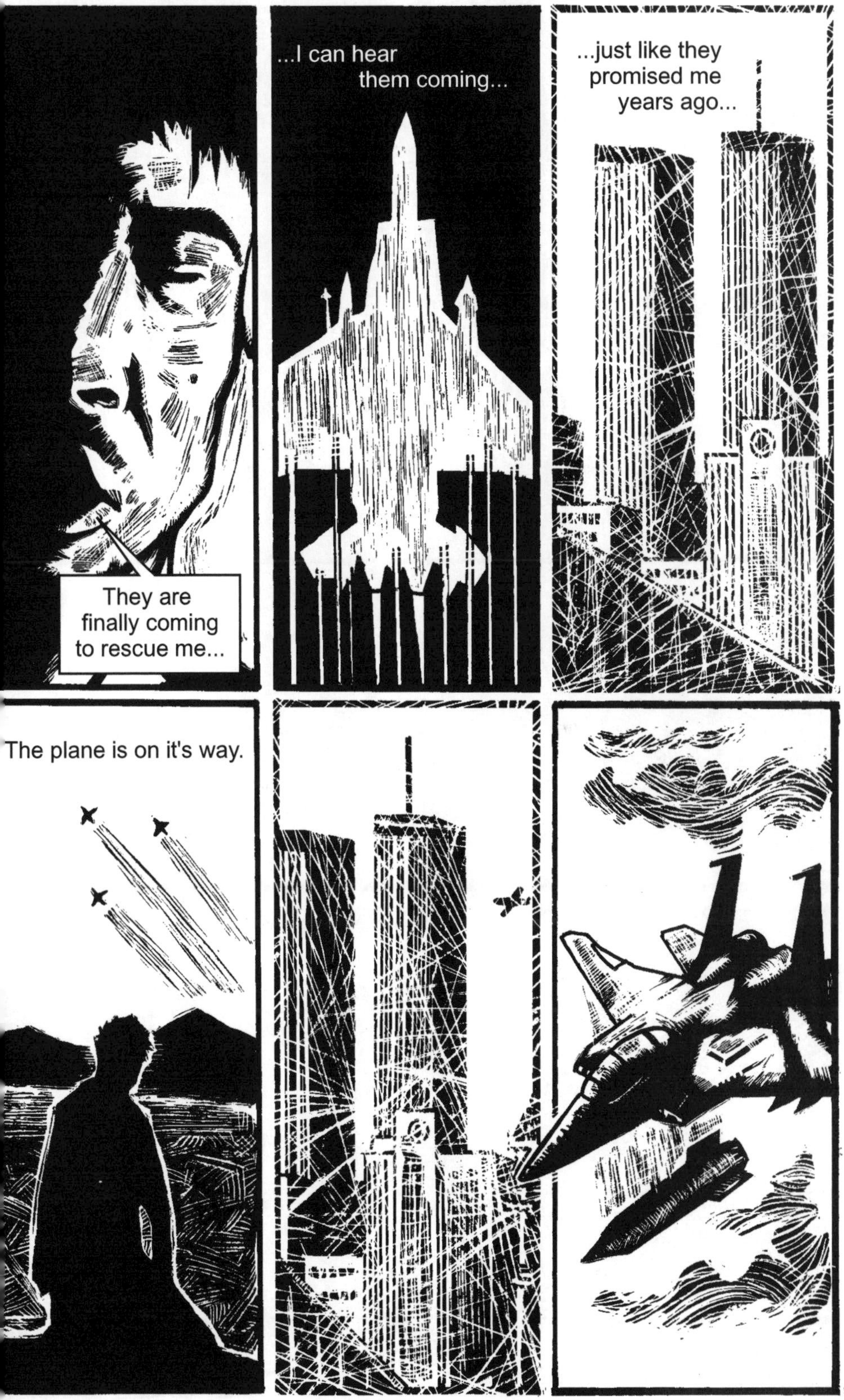
They are finally coming to rescue me...
...I can hear them coming...
...just like they promised me years ago...
The plane is on it's way.

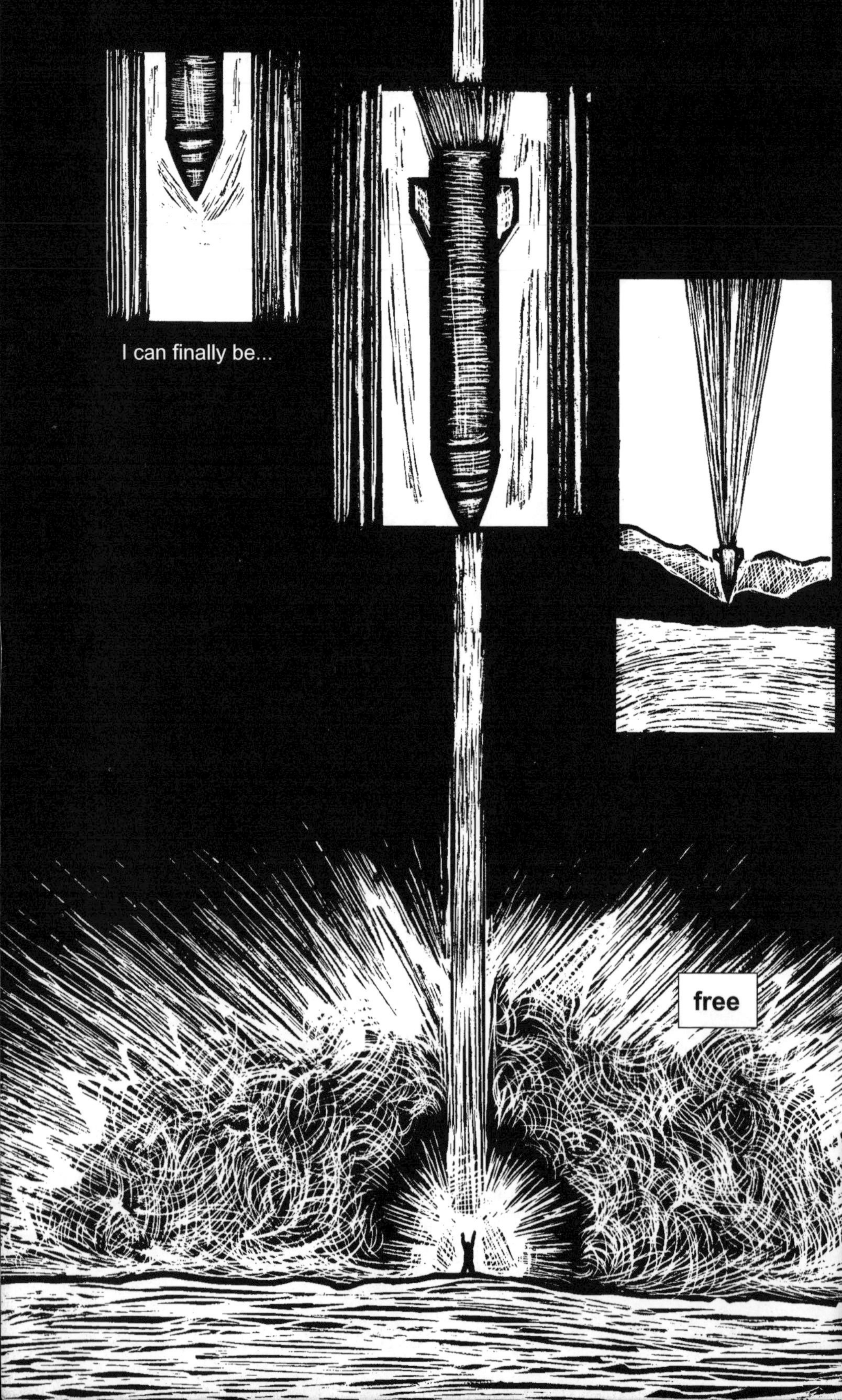
I can finally be...
free